# THE HEAT OF BATTLE

Men and horses were struck by the shells. The animals which had not been hit displayed alarm and fright at the sudden noises. In a moment, the four lines of blue-clad riders were disrupted and thrown into utter confusion.

Before Dusty could start to rise, he felt something strike the bush which was covering him and a musket ball fanned his cheek in passing. Ignoring the thought of how close he had come to being struck by one of his companions' missiles, he hurled aside the foliage and thrust himself erect.

"Yeeah! Texas Light!" Dusty bellowed, hands flashing down and across to draw the matched Army Colts.

Hurdling over the rock, Dusty swung up and fired his right-hand Colt. He sent its bullet into the first sergeant's chest. Rocking backwards on the saddle, the Yankee non-com let his carbine fall and slid after it. However, Dusty knew he could not hope to deal with the second would-be killer...

## J. T. EDSON'S
## FLOATING OUTFIT
## WESTERN ADVENTURES

THE YSABEL KID
SET TEXAS BACK ON HER FEET
THE HIDE AND TALLOW MEN
TROUBLED RANGE
SIDEWINDER
McGRAW'S INHERITANCE
THE BAD BUNCH
TO ARMS, TO ARMS, IN DIXIE!
HELL IN THE PALO DURO
GO BACK TO HELL
THE SOUTH WILL RISE AGAIN
.44 CALIBER MAN
A HORSE CALLED MOGOLLON
GOODNIGHT'S DREAM
FROM HIDE AND HORN
THE HOODED RIDERS
QUIET TOWN
TRAIL BOSS
WAGONS TO BACKSIGHT
RANGELAND HERCULES
THE HALF BREED
THE WILDCATS
THE FAST GUNS
CUCHILO
A TOWN CALLED YELLOWDOG
THE TROUBLE BUSTERS
THE LAW OF THE GUN

THE PEACEMAKERS
THE RUSHERS
THE QUEST FOR BOWIE'S BLADE
THE FORTUNE HUNTERS
THE TEXAN
THE RIO HONDO KID
RIO GUNS
GUN WIZARD
TRIGGER FAST
RETURN TO BACKSIGHT
THE MAKING OF A LAWMAN
TERROR VALLEY
APACHE RAMPAGE
THE RIO HONDO WAR
THE FLOATING OUTFIT
THE MAN FROM TEXAS
GUNSMOKE THUNDER
THE SMALL TEXAN
THE TOWN TAMERS
GUNS IN THE NIGHT
WHITE INDIANS
WACO'S DEBT
OLD MOCCASINS ON THE TRAIL
THE HARD RIDERS
THE GENTLE GIANT
THE TRIGGER MASTER
THE TEXAS ASSASSIN

## J. T. EDSON'S
## CIVIL WAR SERIES

THE COLT AND THE SABRE
THE DEVIL GUN
THE REBEL SPY
UNDER THE STARS AND BARS

KILL DUSTY FOG!
THE BIG GUN
REBEL VENGEANCE (*coming in November*)

# J.T. Edson

## THE BIG GUN

CHARTER BOOKS, NEW YORK

This Charter book contains the complete
text of the original edition.
It has been completely reset in a typeface
designed for easy reading and was printed
from new film.

THE BIG GUN

A Charter Book/published by arrangement with
Transworld Publishers, Ltd.

PRINTING HISTORY
Corgi edition published 1973
Charter edition/September 1987

ISBN: 0-441-06022-6

Charter Books are published by The Berkley Publishing Group,
200 Madison Avenue, New York, NY 10016.
The name "Charter" and the "C" logo
are trademarks belonging to
Charter Communications, Inc.
PRINTED IN THE UNITED STATES OF AMERICA

10 9 8 7 6 5 4 3 2 1

*For Brian F. Barker, who looks like a young Brady Anchor.*

*Author's note:* While complete in itself, this book continues the story begun in *Rebel Vengeance*.

# CHAPTER ONE

## I'm Going to Give You a Chance

Grasping Conrad Blucher by the arms, Privates Block and Grilpan dragged him across the hall and into the dining-room. As Mama Lukie turned from where she had been about to lower and extinguish the crystal chandelier, the burly, blue-clad soldiers flung their captive to the floor.

"Massa Con—!" the Negress began, her fat face showing alarm and concern.

"Get the hell out of here, Mama!" Block commanded and swung his heavy boot hard against Blucher's ribs. "Stay put, you peckerwood* son-of-a-bitch. The major's going to want to talk to you when he comes."

"What's all this ab—?" Mama Lukie commenced indignantly. "You can't do things like that to Massa Con—"

"You heard me, you old bitch!" bawled the black-haired and bearded soldier, swinging towards the massive woman. "Get the hell out of here."

Throwing a glare which would have terrified practically every Negro in that part of Arkansas, Mama Lukie stalked with considerable majesty out of the room. The soldiers watched her go, grinning at each other, then turned their attention to the man on the floor.

Dazed, his face bloody, Blucher crouched against the side-piece and rubbed his ribs where the kick had landed. He was thickset, middle-sized and in his late forties. Going by his now rumpled suit, the shirt—from which the collar and cravat had been torn when he was captured—and Hersome gaiter boots, he was a fairly prosperous businessman of some kind.

* Peckerwood: derogatory name for a Confederate supporter.

1

Still massaging his ribs, for the kick had not been light, Blucher looked about him. He saw most of the familiar sights which he might have expected on a visit to his old friend Eli Cable's home. The long table, at which Blucher had frequently dined, was set for two people. Overhead, the chandelier, mate to the one which illuminated the entrance hall, was still throwing out its light. None of the pictures, furnishings, or other treasures of the room were missing. In fact, everything looked as neat and orderly as when Eli's first wife or—after her death—young Harriet had run the household. That figured. Even if Eli's second wife had not proven as efficient a house-manager as her predecessor, Mama Lukie and her husband Oscar—the family's butler—could be counted on to maintain the expected high standards.

The Yankees had neither looted nor despoiled Cable Grange, Blucher decided at the conclusion of his examination. Of course, going by what he had seen and heard from some of the Negro workers before he had been jumped by the sentries, the Union's Army of Arkansas had good reason for holding on to the property. Possibly the officer in command of the detachment was a man of taste and wished to continue living in style.

The sound of feet on the stairs, followed by a short conversation between Mama Lukie and an educated, if arrogant male, Northern voice, drove the thoughts from Blucher's head. The Negress commenced a protest against the behaviour of the sentries, but was halted by the man on the stairs and ordered to leave the rest of the work until morning. Then the footsteps continued across the hall, approaching the double doors of the dining-room.

The man who entered was tall, wide-shouldered and slim-waisted. Apart from an expression of hard arrogance, that a thick black moustache and tight lips tended to emphasize, he was very handsome. With his curly hair and excellent physique, he would catch the eye in any crowd and many women might find him attractive. He had on a white silk shirt, open to display a bare and hairy chest, skin-tight dark blue riding breeches with scarlet stripes down their outer seams, and Hessian boots. As he strode forward, he exhibited the posture of a horse-soldier, but the colour of the breeches' stripes implied that he belonged to the Union Army's Artillery.

"What's all this, Block?" the newcomer demanded brusquely.

"We caught this peckerwood bastard sneaking around and talking to the niggers, sir," the bigger of the privates replied.

"You did, huh?" Major Kade F. Lyle purred, studying the dishevelled civilian with no more interest and less compassion than a farmer might have displayed towards a worthless animal. "Stand up, man. What do you have to say for yourself, damn it?"

"I—," Blucher began, slowly easing himself on to his feet and standing with his back to the side-piece.

"You can start by telling me who you are," Lyle suggested icily, stroking at his moustache with the knuckle of his left forefinger.

"My name is Conrad Blucher and I own the *Perry County News*—"

"A Secessionist newspaperman, huh?" Lyle sniffed and his tone implied that there could be nothing lower. "And what brought you out here on Nimrod Lake, newspaperman? Were you looking for a story of Union Army atrocities against helpless civilians, or spying for your cowardly Rebel soldiers who've run away and left you?"

"Neither," the civilian answered once more fingering his ribs. "I came up the river to visit Eli Cable and his family."

"You came over twenty miles, just on a social call?" Lyle sneered. His whole bearing was mocking and derisive, but under it was a very real menace and a suggestion of natural cruelty. "That *was* real neighbourly of you."

Blucher looked warily from the major to the two privates. Their kepis, tunics and trousers bore evidence that they too were members of the Artillery; but there was a hard look about their surly features which was alarming. There was hostility and menace on the enlisted men's faces, mingled with an eagerness to inflict pain.

From what the newspaperman had seen in the workshop, the Yankees had good reason for wanting their affairs to remain a secret. However, unless he was no judge of character, all three of them would have had similar attitudes even if there had been nothing of importance happening.

Ever since the sheer weight of numbers opposing the Confederate States' Army of Arkansas and North Texas had forced it to withdraw to the south and west, there had been rumours of strange happenings in Cable Grange. Knowing something of Eli Cable's experiments, Blucher had grown curious. So he had finally—and against his wife's advice—decided to visit the Grange and find out what, if anything, was taking place.

Brought up the Fourche la Fave River by two Negro oarsmen, Blucher had studied the island upon which—at considerable expense—Eli Cable had built his home and workshop. Everything had appeared pretty much as usual; except for a pair of massive Vandenburg Volley guns which were positioned to sweep the sturdy bridge that connected the island with the northern shore of Lake Nimrod. There had been the usual boats drawn up above the water's edge, but no signs of guards. While the comfortable houses of the Negro workers were mostly in darkness, there had been lights upstairs and down at the large, Colonial-style main building.

Deciding against approaching the bridge, for its end was illuminated by fires blazing in basket-like iron cressets and the cabin close to it was clearly occupied, Blucher had landed on the south side of the island. At the workshop he had come across Cable's foreman; a brawny, intelligent Negro called Beckett. Before the two Yankee soldiers had arrived and captured Blucher, using far more force than had been necessary, he had gathered a fair amount of alarming and distressing information.

Somehow, from his scrutiny of the three soldiers' expressions, Blucher did not think they would take kindly to learning the extent of his discoveries. Being a poker player of some proficiency, he tried to school his features into an innocent and disarming expression.

"I've known the Cables for years," the civilian said. "And, as they haven't been down to Perryville for some time, I thought I'd come along and find out if they were all right."

"And what made you think they wouldn't be all right?" Lyle challenged.

"Nothing particularly," Blucher lied, yet with an air of telling the truth. "I just felt puzzled when none of the family came into Perryville for supplies or anything."

"Then why didn't you come to the front of the island, instead of sneaking in the back way?" the major demanded and his attitude implied that he had trapped his victim.

"It's easier—and safer—to land at the rear," Blucher countered, confident that he could prove the statement. "The river's main channel comes by the front. As *you* know, there's a fairly strong current and a steep bank on either side of the bridge. So everybody who comes by boat lands around the back."

"And your only intention was to visit your friends, the Cables, and make sure that they are all right?" Lyle asked.

"That's all," the civilian confirmed and, once again, he had the appearance of complete honesty.

"Then why did you go to the workshop instead of coming straight to the house?" Lyle snapped.

"I saw lights in it and went to see if Eli was working late," Blucher replied, deftly avoiding another trap. "He usually keeps a jug of corn there."

"You went inside?" Lyle asked.

"I didn't need to," Blucher answered evasively. "Beckett came out. Your men attacked me before we could do more than greet each other."

"Well?" Lyle growled, glancing at the soldiers.

"They was talking outside when we catched him, major," Grilpan confirmed reluctantly. "But we don't know how long he'd been there."

Watching the civilian during the conversation, Lyle had grown more angry at his failure to establish that the other was lying, or possessed knowledge of what was being done on the island. Yet Blucher may have seen the device in the workshop. In which case, he probably had sufficient imagination to assess its full potential. Possibly, too, the Negro foreman had given Blucher information on other matters which Lyle would have preferred to remain a secret.

There was far too much at stake for Lyle to want word of his activities to reach the Confederate States' Army. Although he had not taken an active part in the campaign, he had drawn conclusions from what he had heard when talking to other officers. The Rebels' retreat had been more of a carefully planned and executed withdrawal than a rout, followed by a panic-stricken flight. So they might still be—in fact, probably were—a force to be reckoned with. He had too much respect for the raiding abilities of the Southrons' Cavalry to want them to learn what he was doing.

Nor, if it came to that, Lyle any wish for his superiors to make a premature discovery of his intentions. An ambitious, unscrupulous man, he meant to lay the foundations of a great and prosperous future upon the work he had in hand. So he felt disinclined to take chances. Especially when the prevention offered so few difficulties.

All Lyle had to do was dispose of the intruder. He could have Blucher shot as a spy and doubted that "Cussing" Culver would delve too deeply on receiving a report of the incident. The commanding general of the Army of Arkansas most probably would have too many other worries to be concerned about the death of an obscure Southron newspaper owner.

The only thing left to decide was how to arrange the killing. An idea came to Lyle's mind; one which would offer him some enjoyment and pleasure, as well as guarding against possible repercussions at a later date. He had no faith in the loyalty, or honesty, of his enlisted men. So, with an eye on his future, he did not intend to leave himself open to attempts at blackmail, or other pressures to remain silent regarding the incident. He must remove Blucher in a way that could not be turned against him in a few years' time, when the hatreds of the War Between The States had died down, and which would also serve as a warning to the two privates that he was not a safe man to cross. Fortunately, he had everything available to do this. All that remained to do was for him to set the scene.

"Do you know what I think you are?" Lyle inquired, in a voice that was dripping with icy politeness.

"What?" Blucher said warily.

"A liar," Lyle declared, spitting out each word deliberately. "A *liar* and a lousy, cowardly, sneaking Secessionist spy."

"Under the circumstances," Blucher gritted, angry despite himself, indicating the two soldiers, "it doesn't take much courage to make such a statement."

"You mean to suggest that I wouldn't have dared to say it if my men weren't here to protect me?" Lyle suggested, satisfied that his plan was working and the civilian had snapped at his bait.

Suddenly, with a flash of intuition, Blucher had an inkling of what was happening. He had once seen a professional duellist provoking a challenge and the conversation had followed similar lines. There was, he realized, only one thing to do. Play along with the Yankee and hope for a chance to fight back.

"I mean that I'm in no position to give you the only answer a gentleman knows for such an accusation," Blucher replied, forcing himself to remain calm. "If I wasn't your prisoner, I wouldn't be compelled to swallow your insults."

"You mean that you'd call me out under your famous Southron Code Duello?" Lyle asked, the mocking expression growing more pronounced.

"That's just what I'd do," Blucher confirmed. "But I wonder if you'd have the guts to accept, Yankee?"

"*That* is soon settled," Lyle declared and he could not hide the triumph that came with the words. "As the challenged party, I believe I have the choice of weapons?"

"You do," the civilian conceded.

"Then these are my terms," Lyle said. "We'll face each other along the table, each with a revolver lying before us. At the count of three, we each pick it up and fire. Is that acceptable to you?"

"It is," Blucher answered, doubting if he would be given any other choice even if he disagreed and, as far as he could see, the terms were fair enough. "I don't have a revolver, but I expect you have the answer to that."

"I have," Lyle replied. "Block, go and fetch the pistol box from the dressing-table in my quarters."

"Yo!" growled the bearded soldier and slouched out of the room.

Silence dropped after Block had taken his departure. Lyle stood aloof, watching the civilian and hoping to detect some trace of fear or anxiety. In this he was disappointed, for Blucher was a man of considerable courage. Private Grilpan was a morose, bitter man who rarely spoke and, anyway, knew that his superior did not encourage idle conversation with the enlisted men.

For his part, Blucher spent the period of Block's absence wondering what fate had in store for him. He knew that there was little hope of leaving the island alive. Having reconciled himself to that fact, he was grateful for the opportunity—no matter how slight—of being able to make a fight for his life before he was killed. While there was life, there was also hope. Perhaps he might survive and be able to carry a warning to the Confederate States' Army of Arkansas and North Texas. He had no idea how they were faring, but believed that they might cease to retreat once they had crossed the Ouachita River. If so, they would be faced by the peril created from Eli Cable's inventions.

At that moment, Block returned carrying an oblong mahogany box which he placed on the table. Without speaking, Lyle walked over and raised the box's lid. Following him, Blucher saw that it held two very fine English Tranter Army revolvers and their accessories. The weapons, .44 in calibre, had five and seven-eighths inch long octagonal barrels, double-action mechanisms, no cocking spur on the hammers and straighter, less hand-fitting butts than those of an Army or Navy Colt. There were brass percussion caps on the nipples of the cylinders and the chambers which showed above the recessed bottom of the box had round lead balls, covered with a coating of grease to prevent the danger of a multiple discharge, in them.

"Choose the one you want, they're both equally lethal,"

Lyle said, almost politely. "Then Block will put it on the table for you. As you see, *I* don't intend to take any unfair advantage."

"Neither will I," Blucher stated and indicated the upper weapon. "I'll take that one."

"Let him see that all the chambers are loaded and capped, Block," Lyle ordered and, after that had been done, continued to Blucher. "Are you satisfied?"

"I am," answered the civilian, for every chamber appeared to be in a firing condition.

"Then we'll make a start," Lyle declared, extracting the second Tranter. "I don't want to be up all night."

Following Block, the civilian watched him lay the revolver on the table with its butt towards him. As the soldier went to join his companion by the side-piece, Blucher was tempted to snatch up the weapon and start shooting. Two things stopped him from doing so. He was a Southron gentleman, reared in an exacting code of honourable behaviour. And, at the other end of the table, Lyle watched him with alert, somewhat mocking eyes, and still held the revolver. Stepping into position, Blucher raised his right hand and let it hover about six inches over Tranter's fancy rosewood butt.

When satisfied that the other man did not intend to snatch up the weapon prematurely, Lyle laid down his own and lifted away his hand.

"Count to five, Block," the major said. "And, when he reaches it, we both pick up our weapons then start to fire."

"One!" the soldier obliged, watching the men at the table with the cruel anticipation of a spectator awaiting the start of a dog-, or a snake-fight.*

Gazing along the table, Lyle felt a growing surge of savage, exultant excitement. It was a sensation he had experienced on two previous occasions when he had contrived to cause similar situations. Twice, before his enlistment, he had fought illicit duels and had emerged victorious; due to the thought and special training which he

---

* A description of a snake-fight is given in *The Colt and the Sabre*.

had put in to ensure that he had a much better than even chance of winning.

"Two!" Block said.

Would Blucher allow the full count before grabbing at the Tranter? Lyle asked himself. Groendaul, the second victim, had only let it reach three. Not that his treachery had saved him. Being a Southron, Blucher would most likely stick to the rules; for all the good that would do him.

"Three!"

Watching Lyle and listening to the count, Blucher was also thinking fast. Everything seemed fair enough on the surface. As the Yankee officer had given him first choice, the weapons must both be correctly loaded. Undoubtedly Lyle must be a very good, capable shot, but so was Blucher. So, if he could shoot the major, he might have a chance to escape. Neither of the enlisted men had a firearm, having left their Spencer repeating rifles by the front door when they had dragged him in. With that much distance separating him from them, he ought to be able to drop both and flee. Once clear of the house, he would make a run for the boats. If he was lucky enough to get away, he would head for the Ouachita River in the hope of contacting Confederate troops and warn them of the dangers they would soon be facing.

"Four!"

Suddenly Blucher became aware of how Lyle was looking at him. No shadow of concern or doubt marred the major's handsome face. Rather it bore an expression of complete, self-satisfied confidence and even a hint of sadistic, perverted pleasure. That he, apparently, had no wish to take an unfair advantage showed in his hand being raised a good foot above the Tranter.

Why did Lyle look so confident? Blucher wondered.

It almost seemed that the Yankee knew that he must win!

What could be wrong?

Was there some trickery involved in the loading of the revolvers?

"Five!"

On the word, two hands dipped toward the table!

Although Blucher had the shorter distance to reach, he was disturbed by what he had seen and the train of doubts that it had aroused. So he fumbled a little as his fingers met the unfamiliar, awkward shape of the Tranter's butt. Even as he raised it, he knew that he was going to be too late.

Smoothly, moving with the speed which implied long training, Lyle scooped up his revolver. His left hand joined the right, closing over it and helping to support the weight of the gun. Along the length of the table, he knew better than to try to shoot by instinctive alignment. So he elevated his weapon to shoulder level, sighting along the barrel and squeezing the trigger. Flame spurted and the bullet was flung into the centre of Blucher's chest. Knocked staggering, he lost his hold on the Tranter. That did not save him any more than the fact that he was already mortally wounded.

Bearing his teeth in a wolfish leer of sheer animal delight at inflicting pain, Lyle corrected his aim and fired again. The second bullet passed into the centre of the civilian's forehead and burst its way out of the back of his skull. Already off balance, he twirled on his heels and measured his length face down on the floor.

"That got the bastard!" Block enthused.

"Go and keep those damned niggers out of here!" Lyle snarled, lowering his Tranter and looking at the enlisted men.

Even as Grilpan hurried away, footsteps sounded beyond the door. They were light, suggestive of feminine high heels descending the stairs. Passing the soldier in the doorway, a beautiful woman entered the room. She had a flimsy robe thrown hurriedly over a diaphanous nightdress, which revealed far more than it concealed, and high-heeled slippers graced her feet. All in all, from her blonde hair to her toes, she was a very shapely, voluptuous creature and her slinking gait added to her allure. There was a golden wedding ring on the appropriate finger.

"Kade, what's happening?" the woman began, then her eyes went to the body as it lay oozing blood over the carpet. "Oh my God! Wha—Who—?"

"Get out of here, Monica!" Lyle growled, displaying

little concern over the revulsion and shock which she was clearly experiencing. "I'll be up in a minute and tell you."

"But what's going on?" the blonde croaked, her face pallid as she turned her gaze from the corpse.

"I'll tell you when I come up!" the officer shouted, annoyed at the way Block was eyeing the woman. "Suppose somebody was to see you down here?"

"You sent your man to keep the servants away," the woman pointed out. "And Harriet's locked in her room. Why can't you let me—?"

"Because I said for you to go!" Lyle replied. "This's no place for you and I'll come up as soon as I get through here."

"Oh, all right," the blonde sniffed petulantly, knowing better than to try his patience too far. "I'll go. Don't be too long."

With that the woman turned and stalked from the room. She was conscious of Block watching her every motion and, to annoy Lyle, increased the lascivious rolling of her buttocks until beyond his range of vision. Ascending the stairs, she looked back at the entrance to the dining-room.

If Monica Cable had been less interested in what might be going on to her rear, she could have noticed that the door of the room next to her own was open a short way. Before she had turned her attention to the front, it was closed and she went by without knowing that she had been observed.

Having closed the door silently, preventing her stepmother from realizing that she too was able to leave the room after having been locked in for the night, Harriet Cable stood glaring at it for a moment. She realized that Mama Lukie had been correct when suggesting that something was going on between Monica and Major Lyle. That was now obvious from the freedom with which the blonde moved around the house. Previously, Harry—as her friends mostly called her—had tended to discount the old Negress's hints on grounds of jealousy. Mama Lukie had been devoted to Harry's mother and had never become reconciled to Eli Cable remarrying, especially to a woman like Monica.

Well, at last the truth was out.

While Harry had obtained a spare key for her door from Mama Lukie, she knew the Negress would never have given one to Monica. Which meant that Mrs. Cable was not kept a prisoner at night. Perhaps she was even a willing hostage and had used Eli Cable's love for her as a means of ensuring his compliance with the Yankee major's demands.

"It could have been she who told Lyle about Big Minnie and Pulling Sue," Harry mused, recalling that there had been a number of puzzling aspects about the Union soldiers' arrival at Cable Grange. Her father had kept his work a secret, yet they had seemed to know all about it; including a couple of very recent developments. "That settles it. I'm going to tell Poppa what's happening."

Locking the door, so as to avoid arousing suspicion if anybody checked up on her, Harry crossed to the wardrobe. Slipping out of her nightgown, she opened the door and stood naked before the full-length mirror. It reflected the image of a small, buxom, yet firm-fleshed girl of eighteen. Not as out-and-out beautiful as her stepmother, maybe, but quite pretty in a friendly, open way that hinted at a normally merry nature. Her brunette hair was curly and cropped short in defiance to the fashion of the day.

Although Harry had been disinclined to accept Mama Lukie's conclusions regarding her mother, more from a naturally charitable nature than for any feeling of affection, she had gathered the means to escape if the need arose. Taking clothing from the wardrobe, she made ready for her departure.

Donning her underwear, Harry followed it with a boy's dark grey shirt, yellowish-brown Nankeen trousers, thick grey woolen socks and riding boots. A wolfskin coat and a low-crowned, wide-brimmed black hat completed her attire.

Opening her dressing-table's drawer, she dug under its contents and produced a present from her father on her fifteenth birthday. Opening the box, she removed the four inch barrelled, ivory-handled Colt 1849 Pocket Pistol. Her room had not been searched by the Yankees, probably because Monica did not know of the revolver, so it was still available for her to use.

Knowing that the weapon was loaded and capped, she dropped it into the jacket's right pocket. Into the left, she stuffed the powder flask, cap box, nipple-wrench, a small tin holding deer's grease and a buckskin bag containing a supply of round .31 calibre lead bullets.

Armed and equipped, if in a somewhat scanty, Spartan fashion, the girl doused her room's light. Going to the window, she raised its sash and looked out. There was no sign of activity on the part of the Yankees. So she eased herself over the sill. A section of sturdy lattice-work ran down the wall, thickly covered by a Virginia creeper. Always a tomboy, Harry had frequently used it as a means of leaving the house unseen.

On reaching the ground, she looked back at the house. Nobody raised the alarm and she hurried towards Mama Lukie's quarters.

About an hour later, accompanied by the Negress's youngest son, Eric, Harry sat in a boat and passed along the lake towards the Fourche la Fave River. A supply of food lay between them and she hoped that they would be able to obtain horses in Perryville. Then she would try to reach her father and tell him of how he had been tricked into putting a powerful, dangerous weapon into the hands of the Yankees.

## CHAPTER TWO

## You Don't Want to Get Killed

"Come on, you Yankee bastards!" Corporal Kiowa Cotton breathed, as he crouched between two bushes and watched the pair of Union Army sentries talking. "Quit that jaw-flapping and do your son-of-a-bitching duty like soldiers."

Tall, lean, Indian-dark, with a high cheek-boned, hook-nosed face that was suggestive of mixed blood, Kiowa Cotton looked—and was—a very dangerous man to have as an enemy. On his head of close-cropped black hair, he had a yellow-topped kepi. The silver star-in-a-circle badge—the circle bearing a laurel wreath motif and the centre of the star embossed with the letters TLC —that usually graced the hat's front had been removed as an aid to remaining undetected. A tight-rolled red bandana trailed its long ends over the front of his waist-length, cadet-grey tunic. His yellow-striped riding breeches ended in the leggings of Kiowa moccasins. Around his waist hung a Western-style gunbelt. At the left side, butt forward for a cross-draw, was holstered a Remington 1861 Army revolver. The sheath on the right side of the belt was empty, for the bowie knife—its blade blackened by smoke to prevent it from glinting and maybe attracting unwanted attention—was in his right hand and ready for use.

Instead of heeding Kiowa's silent exhortation, the sentries continued to talk. Waiting somewhat impatiently for them to separate and go where they could be dealt with, the sergeant looked around the large clearing. Once again, he decided that it should never have been selected as a camp-site for such an important man; particularly when he was traveling with so small an escort.

In times of peace, the clearing would have been a pleasant place in which to spend a night. Being on the banks of a small stream that eventually flowed into the Ouachita River, one could easily catch fish for supper. The surrounding woods gave shelter from the wind and the Pine Bluff-Arkadelphia trail was near by.

Those very qualities, particularly the latter, made the clearing anything but an ideal resting place in times of war. The trees and bushes that lined three of its sides, including a scattering along the banks of the stream, gave cover in which enemies could—in fact, at that moment *did*—find concealment.

Along the edge of the trail, again offering a hiding place for a member of the Texas Light Cavalry, were parked a Concord coach and two Rocker ambulances.\* At the centre of the clearing, the large camp-fire was gradually dying down since all the soldiers not on guard duty had retired to their two-men pup-tents. The wagons' teams and horses of the escort were picketed in two lines parallel to the stream, watched over by a third sentry. The pair being studied by Kiowa shared the remainder of the boundary between them. One went from the wagons, north around the perimeter until making contact with the man on the picket line. Moving south, the other would approach the corporal's hiding place. If permitted, he could turn east and pass behind the brightly-lit marquee which alone showed any sign of life. Inside, "Cussing" Culver, commanding general of the Union's Army of Arkansas, was entertaining the officers of his company-strong escort and three civilians.

The latter group, particularly General Culver, was the reason for Kiowa Cotton's presence and desire that the sentries should continue with their patrols instead of standing in conversation.

The Battle of Martin's Mill had been fought four days earlier. By winning it, the Confederate States' Army of Arkansas and North Texas had succeeded in moving all their supplies and equipment south across the Ouachita

---

\* A more detailed description of a Rocker ambulance is given in *Hound Dog Man*.

River. While the rest of the army was consolidating their
position along the bank of the Ouachita, Company "C" of
the Texas Light Cavalry— under its newly-promoted commanding officer, Captain Dustine Edward Marsden Fog—
had been sent north of the river to reconnoitre.

On their way back, with information regarding the Yankees' troop dispositions, Kiowa Cotton—ranging ahead as
scout—had seen the camp being set up in the clearing.
Moving closer undetected had been an easy task for a man
schooled in the demanding arts of Indian fighting. Unseen
and unsuspected, the corporal had studied the clearing and
its occupants. The escort was a full company of the Long
Island Lancers, a fancy volunteer outfit led by Eastern
dudes, and they were guarding old "Cussing" Culver himself.

When Captain Dusty Fog had heard Kiowa's news, he
had acted with the kind of swift decision the men of Company "C" had already come to expect of him. There were
no other Union troops in the vicinity, so he had decided
that they would try to capture the general. Carefully, but
thoroughly, he had made his plans based on Kiowa's description of the terrain and the clearing's lay out. Several of
Dusty's men had been Texas Rangers before enlisting in the
Confederate States' Army. Their duties had chiefly been
concerned with fighting Indians, so he had sufficient soldiers capable of silent stalking to make his scheme possible. Selecting the best of the ex-Rangers, he had assigned
them to the duty of silencing the sentries. The rest of Company "C," less those assigned to ride herd on their horses,
were waiting in the woods and ready to move in once the
way was prepared.

When Kiowa had last come into contact with the Long
Island Lancers, during the battle of Martin's Mill,* they
had worn normal U.S. Cavalry uniforms and been armed
with nine foot long, Norwegian fir lances. Handling their
present duty, they had adopted a more fancy attire—copied
from the dress of the British Army's 17th Lancers—sup-

---

* The story of the meeting with the Lancers and of the Battle of
Martin's Mill is told in *Rebel Vengeance*.

plied by the wealthy New York families who had financed, equipped and recruited the regiment. Although lances were piled outside the pup tents, each sentry carried a Spencer carbine in his white gauntlet-covered hands.

The booming tones of General Culver reached Kiowa's ears, describing in a profanity-filled manner how, having driven the Rebels to the Ouachita, he was merely awaiting reinforcements before pushing them from Arkansas and commencing the conquest of Texas.

A faint, savage grin twisted at the corporal's lips as he listened to the bombastic words. Far from being driven, the Army of Arkansas and North Texas had made a satisfactory and carefully executed withdrawal. What was more, if Kiowa knew anything about General Ole Devil Hardin, the Yankees were going to find any further "pushing" to be a mighty difficult and dangerous proposition.

At last the two sentries separated. Carrying his Spencer at a slovenly trail, the closer of them started to stroll towards Kiowa. His companion, with the short repeater across the crook of the left arm, ambled in the opposite direction.

"Damn it!" Kiowa snarled under his breath. "The idle son-of-a-bitch's going *across,* not round!"

Instead of following his previous route, the second sentry was ambling away from the wagons. That would not help the short, white-haired, anything but decrepit, Corporal Vern Hassle to complete his assignment.

The call of a whip-poor-will, repeated twice, came from the picket line. That meant, Kiowa knew, the sentry watching the horses had been dealt with. Apart from a slight restlessness among the animals, there had been nothing to suggest it was happening. Certainly neither of the remaining guards, nor the rest of the camp's occupants appeared to be aware that one of their number had been rendered *hors de combat*.

Oblivious of his own peril, or his companion's fate, the sentry followed the trail until turning along the edge of the clearing. His attention was directed towards the tent, as he tried to hear what was being said. Nor did he take his gaze from the well-illuminated interior. Certainly he did not see the menacing figure crouching as if made of stone amongst the bushes.

Glancing across the clearing towards the wagons, Kiowa found that the second sentry had developed an extra shadow. Grasping a thick branch, Vern Hassle was stalking his victim on silent feet.

As the sentry went by, Kiowa rose. Without making a warning sound, the corporal glided forward. Reaching out with his left hand, he passed it above the near-side brass shoulder scale—which even carried a copy of the 17th Lancers' skull and crossed-bones insignia—of the blue tunic and clapped it over the man's mouth. Stifling any outcry before it could be attempted, Kiowa jerked the lancer's head backwards. At the same instant, his right hand thrust home the bowie knife. Its clip point sank into the man's kidney region. Although he died almost instantly and in silence, the Spencer slipped from his lifeless grasp and dropped to the ground.

Having kept Kiowa's victim under observation, Vern Hassle timed his own attack to coincide with his companion's. Swinging the stout piece of branch parallel to the ground—having decided that the fancy Lancer's cap offered too much protection against a downwards blow—the old-timer crashed it against the base of his objective's skull. Continuing to move with a speed that belied his white hair and years, he followed his victim down. Flattened on the grass behind the motionless sentry, Hassle waited until sure that his actions had gone unnoticed. Then, picking up the Spencer, he wriggled rapidly back to the shadows of the wagons.

There was no sign of life from the pup-tents. Nor did Culver's flow of profane, bombastic chatter cease, to suggest that he had heard the slight disturbance as the sentries were removed. Satisfied, Kiowa gave the call of a whippoor-will twice and Hassle echoed the signal.

Figures flitted through the trees, feeling their way with cautious feet so as to keep the noise of their passage to a minimum. While they might not have succeeded if their opponents had been Indians, they were quiet enough to avoid detection by the Easterners against whom they were operating.

Despite the knowledge that they were not dealing with men who possessed the natural alertness and keen senses of Indians, and that Company "C" had defeated three Companies of Long Island Lancers at the Battle of Martin's Mill, the Texans were too battle-wise to take unnecessary risks or grow over-confident. They had lost several men in the fighting and were outnumbered by the party in the clearing. Only by attaining complete surprise could they hope to achieve their new commanding officer's purpose. Every one of them figured life would be a whole heap easier and more pleasant all round if they did that.

Captain Fog might be very young, hardly more than seventeen, but he possessed a mighty forceful character and it was well to pay heed to his orders or instructions. There was no better gun-handler in the Texas Light Cavalry, for he could draw with lightning speed and shoot *very* accurately with either hand. He had few peers as a horse-master, or in sabre-fighting mounted and a-foot. Using tricks learned from Ole Devil Hardin's "Chinese"* servant, augmented by considerable physical strength, he had proven capable of out-fighting bigger, heavier, older and more powerful men when necessary.

So, when Captain Fog had laid great emphasis on the need for silence and care, the enlisted men had paid greater attention than they would have to an officer who did not stand as high in their esteem.

On reaching the edge of the clearing, the enlisted men halted in concealment. They lined their weapons, revolvers or whatever type of shoulder-arm they might possess, on the tents and waited to see if their presence had been detected. Apparently it had not, for there was no sign of activity on the part of the Yankees.

Satisfied that all had gone to plan, Captain Fog moved towards the marquee. He was accompanied by his second-

---

* Although Tommy Okasi was a native of Japan, the country was so little known in the 1860's that, being Oriental, he was thought by many people to be Chinese.

in-command and the Company's sergeant major. While they were armed with an 1860 Army Colt in each hand, his matched, bone-handled revolvers were still in the cross-draw holsters of his well-designed Western-style gunbelt. Instead, he grasped a long-bladed knife in his right fist.

Inside the marquee, General Culver stood at the head of the collapsible table. A short, broad, bearded man, he his full-dress uniform with an air of belligerent self-assurance. All his comments on the future conduct of the War Between The States, or his part in it, were directed at the trio of Eastern newspapermen.

Culver's words were full of the bluster and obscenities —referred to as "colourful language" by his friends, although others used a different, less complimentary term—which had given him the sobriquet, "Cussing." They were designed to divert attention from what he—and the Lancers' officers—knew to have been his failure. Despite all his previous boasting, the Rebels had withdrawn —which was far different from having been chased or driven—to the safety of the Ouachita's southern shore. Nor would they be so easy to dislodge from their new positions.

Being aware of the value of a good press—although the term had not yet come into use—to a man with political ambitions, Culver was taking the newspapermen on a tour of the forward areas. To impress them with his courage and ability and to emphasize his control of the situation, he had refused a larger escort. Instead, he had demanded just one company of Lancers, in full dress, and had traveled in considerable luxury.

Being a frugal man by nature, the general had caused the dinner to be served late. With it over, he had contrived to keep his guests from becoming bored or wanting to go to bed; but had avoided expending too much of his liquor stock. There would, he had hinted, be more lavish entertainment once they had returned to Little Rock.

"We didn't have any trouble in running the Rebels back this far," Culver was saying. "And, once we have our reinforcements, we'll chase them clear into their louse-infested, son-of-a-bitching State. I'll make those motherfu—."

While the general was continuing with his often-repeated promise, his striker had been taking a bottle of whiskey from the liquor chest which was part of the marquee's furnishings. The plump, red-faced soldier started to draw the cork, then he saw something shiny thrust through the rear wall. Letting out a startled exclamation, the striker allowed the bottle to slip from his fingers. However, his duties were servant and attendant, not fighter, so he responded too slowly to give a warning that might have been acted upon.

With a slight ripping sound, a razor-sharp knife slashed downwards through the wall of the marquee. The damaged section was torn horizontally and three figures thrust through the gap into the light. They came so swiftly that there was hardly any interval between the insertion of the knife being seen by the striker and their appearance.

At the right of the trio, wearing the uniform of an enlisted man in the Texas Light Cavalry, was a tall, gangling sergeant major. Taken with his prominent Adam's apple, somewhat receding chin and miserable expression, the three chevrons, topped by an arc, denoting his rank seemed out of place. He looked more like a dejected, ill-used sandhill crane than the senior non-commissioned officer of a tough, fighting cavalry Company. However, the gunbelt about his waist had been well-made and the Army Colts in his hands were lined steadily.

To the left was a tall, well-made young first lieutenant. Under his white Jeff Davis campaign hat, which was thrust to the back of his head, was an untidy mop of curly, fiery red hair. He had a good-looking, freckled, pugnaciously cheerful cast of features. Like the sergeant major, he brandished two long barrelled Army Colts with the air of being extremely competent in their use. Apart from having only two half-inch wide, three-inch long gold bars on his tunic's stand up collar and a single gold braid twisted to form a "chicken guts" Austrian knot on his sleeves, his uniform matched that of his commanding officer. The position of his gunbelt's holsters showed that he used the low cavalry twist-hand draw.

Between the two was the young man who had made such an impression upon the hard-bitten, hard-riding, harder-fighting veterans of Company "C" that they were willing to accept his orders without question. A mere youth, in years, but who had already performed deeds that would have taxed the abilities of older, more experienced men.

If one had been expecting a giant, disappointment, incredulity even might have resulted at the first sight of Dusty Fog. He had dusty blond hair and a tanned, moderately handsome face that—in times of peace anyway—did not tend to catch the eye. Although he was no more than five foot six in height, he was anything but puny. His wide shoulders trimmed down to a slim waist in a manner that hinted at considerable strength.

Since assuming command of the Company, after having won promotion in the field for his activities during the Battle of Martin's Mill, Dusty had adopted a somewhat less formal style of dress than had been permitted by the man he had replaced. While his tunic partially conformed to the *Manual of Dress Regulations,* by being double-breasted, with the correct type of stand up collar and twin rows of seven buttons, it lacked the prescribed "skirt extending to half-way between hip and knee." Instead of the formal black silk cravat, he sported a tight-rolled scarlet silk bandana. His riding breeches had the traditional yellow stripe along their outer seams and spurs decorated the heels of his Hessian boots. Since his elevation in rank, he wore *three* collar bars and his "chicken guts" were formed from two lengths of gold braid.

Free from the late Captain von Hertz's restrictions, he no longer used the official weapon belt with its awkward, impractical close-topped holster. The rig he now wore offered him considerably more freedom and allowed for exceptional speed in the drawing of the matched, bone-handled Colt 1860 Army revolvers; as he proceeded to demonstrate.

Even as the occupants of the marquee started to turn, or

stared at the intruders, Dusty dropped the knife and his hand flashed inwards. Crossing, they closed about the butts and swept free the Colts in a flickering blur of motion. With the seven and a half inch "Civilian" pattern barrels* turning to the front, just clear of the holsters' lips, his fore-fingers entered the triggerguards and his thumbs drew back the hammers. Before the knife had reached the ground, both guns were pointing in the direction of the table.

Dusty had never heard of psychology, but he was aware of the value of demonstrating his ambidextrous gun-wizardry. That was why he had elected to slit open the mar-quee's wall and allow his companions to enter with drawn weapons. The speed with which he had produced his Colts was likely to have a numbing effect when seen by men who had not come into contact with a Western-trained gun-fighter.

"No noise, gentlemen!" Dusty warned in a gentle—yet somewhat menacing—Texas drawl, the muzzles of his Colts moved slowly from side to side and seeming to threaten every man before them. "There's a circle of guns around the camp and your sentries're all out of the deal." His right hand weapon halted with its bore directed at the Lancers' major. "Easy there. My men'll kill anybody who comes out of the tents."

Although the major's mouth had been opening and he was tensing to leap at the small Texan, he refrained from doing either. Being a good poker player, he knew that he was not hearing an idle threat or a bluff. He could also visualize the consequences of any action that would arouse the camp. Freshly woken, illuminated by the still burning fire, his men would be at the mercy of the Texans as they emerged from their tents. Nor would lances be of any use against the firearms which would be opposing them. That had been proven all too thoroughly at the Battle of Martin's Mill, when a single Company of the Texas Light Cavalry —perhaps the very one now surrounding the camp—had

---

* Colt 1860 Army revolvers intended for sale to the military had eight inch long barrels.

defeated three companies of the Long Island Lancers. There was only one sensible way to act.

"Stand still, Owen, Stewart!" the major growled at his lieutenants. "They've got us cold."

"That's being *real* sensible," 1st Lieutenant Charles William Henry Blaze—whose fiery thatch of hair had earned him the nickname "Red"—drawled and turned his gaze to the startled civilians. "You fellers're newspapermen, I'd say. So you don't want to get killed before you can write *this* story. Which being the case, don't make a sound."

"What the hell do you want?" Culver demanded, staying half-risen from his chair.

"You, general," Dusty replied and, suddenly, in some strange way, he appeared to have grown. No longer did he look small, young and insignificant; but seemed to be the biggest *man* present. "It's *your* decision. Yell for help, make a fight of it, and there'll be a whole lot more than just you in here get killed. Call the play wrong and you'll lose another company of Lancers."

Although Culver had had a few drinks, they were insufficient to dull his mind. So he was able to understand the full implication of the situation. If he raised the alarm, he would most likely die. Even if he survived and escaped capture, the Lancers would be slaughtered as they came to investigate. There was nothing more sure than that. Young as that *big* blond Texan might be, he was a menacing, commanding figure. Culver could not detect the slightest hesitation, weakness or lack of resolution about him.

Faced with the choice between capture and practically certain death if he attempted to resist, the general thought fast. His career was already under a cloud, due to his failure to prevent the Rebels from reaching safety with all their supplies, equipment and other material. There was to be a court of inquiry into the affair, from which he would be highly unlikely to escape with an unblemished reputation. Perhaps, provided he handled things properly, being captured would give him a way out of his difficulties. It would not help his Army career, of course, but he was thinking of his future as a politician after the War.

"What will you do to my escort if I yield to your demands?" Culver asked, with none of his usual profanity.

Although the general addressed the words to Dusty Fog, who was studying him with level grey eyes and an impassive face, they were heard by the three newspapermen. Culver was unable to resist darting a quick glance at them, hoping to see a favourable reaction. They seemed interested, but he could not be sure what other emotions he had unleashed by his question.

"Not a thing, unless we're driven to it," Dusty promised. "I can't say how bad hurt your sentries are, but we don't want to kill without reason. So we'll take their horses, to make sure they can't follow us. But that's as far as it'll go on our side."

"Our *horses!*" growled the Lancers' second lieutenant, tensing. "Like—"

"Stay put, feller!" Red Blaze advised, thrusting forward his right hand Colt. "Me and this old plough-handle outrank you, so that's an order. Anyway, losing the horses's better than losing all your men. Some of our fellers're toting scatter-guns and they're surely evil."

"Don't make trouble, Stewart!" commanded the major, face red with anger and humiliation. "We're licked!"

While speaking, the major watched the three Texans. He saw nothing to give him hope or comfort. Despite his appearance, that lanky sergeant major handled the two Colts in a skilled manner. If the rest of the Company were equally able, his men would not stand a chance. So, much as he hated to do it, he continued to yield to the inevitable.

"You're sure that nothing worse will happen to the Lancers?" Culver asked, being determined to instil a sense of his concern over the enlisted men's welfare in the civilians' memories.

"You've got my word on it, sir," Dusty declared, guessing what the general was trying to do.

"Then I'll go with you and save their lives," Culver stated and wondered if he should insert a comment to the newspapermen regarding the advisability of such a decision.

After a moment's thought, Culver concluded that he had

said enough. His words would read very well, when they were reported in the newspapers. Instead of being labelled as the general who failed to make good on his boasts, people would think of him as the noble, gallant officer who had been willing to sacrifice his freedom to prevent his soldiers from being killed.

Suddenly Culver became aware of the Rebel captain's scrutiny. There was a faint smile on the young blond's lips. With the sickening force of a kick in the stomach, the general become uncomfortably suspicious that his line of thought was known to his captor.

That was truer than Culver imagined. On learning of Culver's presence with the three civilians, Dusty had guessed what was behind it. So he had taken that aspect into consideration when making his arrangements. He had gambled on Culver, faced with the consequences of failure, being willing to gain some acclaim if given the chance. From what had happened, Dusty's summation was correct. However, he refused to let a sense of triumph make him careless.

"Lie face down on the floor, gentlemen," the small Texan said, indicating the lieutenants.

"Do it!" the major gritted when his subordinates showed an inclination towards refusal.

"And you'd best come to the door of the tent, major," Dusty suggested, as his order was obeyed. "I want you to call out your guard commander and see that anybody else who shows knows what's happening."

"All right," the major sighed, watching his captor for any hint of carelessness and failing to find it.

While Dusty supervised the major, standing just too far away for there to be any danger of being tackled by him, Sergeant Major Billy Jack backed to the torn wall of the tent. At his signal, three enlisted men entered. They were told to disarm the lieutenants, then gather up Culver's traveling gear.

"You gents stay peaceable and you'll not get hurt," Red told the newspapermen.

"Count on us for that," declared one of the trio. "Like

you said, I'd hate to get killed before I've written *this* story."

"Talking about the story," the second newspaperman went on, "what's your captain's name?"

"It's Dusty Fog," Red replied, full of pride in his cousin's success. "Likely you'll be hearing it plenty from now on."

## CHAPTER THREE

## This is as Far as We Go

General Jackson Baines Hardin had the tanned, lean and hardy look of a born fighting man. Black haired, just touched with grey at the temples, his face had a slightly Mephistophelian aspect which partly accounted for his sobriquet, "Ole Devil." He was a complete contrast to his captured counterpart in the Union Army. There was none of Culver's bombast and profanity in Ole Devil's bearing or speech. Intelligent, morally and physically courageous, capable, tolerant and understanding—if inclined to be harsh and ruthless when confronted by stupidity or inefficiency—he had the saving graces of breeding, modesty and a sense of humour.

The men of the Confederate States' Army of Arkansas and North Texas admired, respected and trusted Ole Devil, although he had but recently assumed command. It had been due to his excellent planning and superb leadership that they had completed their successful withdrawal to south of the Ouachita River.

Standing on the judge's rostrum, with his feet spread slightly apart, Ole Devil presented a commanding, imposing figure. In a subtle way he was paying tribute to the quality of his audience by having taken special care with his appearance.

A white Jeff Davis campaign hat rested squarely on his head. He had fastened back the lapels of his cadet-grey, double-breasted full dress coat to the top button in each row of eight which narrowed from four inches apart to three inches at the bottom. That exposed his white shirt's collar and a black silk cravat fastened in the fashion of a bow-tie. The stand-up collar—bearing the three gold stars encircled by a laurel wreath insignia of his rank—the cuffs of his sleeves and fringed waist-sash were of cavalry yellow. His "chicken guts" were formed from four strands of gold braid, being further indications of his status as were the two strips of gold braid— $\frac{5}{8}''$ wide and $\frac{1}{8}''$ apart—along the outer seams of his riding breeches. Over the waist-sash was buckled a well-polished black weapon belt that supported a horse-soldier's sabre at the left and had a revolver holstered butt forward on the right. Highly-shone Hessian boots, with glittering spurs on their heels, completed his smart uniform.

Despite its proximity to the enemy, the court house at Arkadelphia—seat of Clark County, Arkansas—was crowded with grey-uniformed officers. It was possible to distinguish in which branch of the service they were employed by the colour of their collars, cuffs, trousers' stripes and, where applicable, the tops of their kepis. Infantry, blue; Artillery, red; Cavalry, yellow; Medical, black; Engineers and Staff; buff.

Occupying the front row of seats were the colonels and lieutenant colonels who commanded Ole Devil's regiments. Their exact status could be established most easily by respectively three, or two, gold stars on their collars. Majors showed only one star, but their sleeves also carried triple gold braid Austrian knots to show that they held field rank. Next came the majors and senior captains; the leaders of the companies or batteries in the colonels' outfits.

Slowly Ole Devil swept his gaze around the room, reading interest, speculation and anticipation in every face. Probably they had already guessed at his reason for gathering them together and were eagerly waiting to discover exactly what the future held in store for them. His news would surprise many, please some but disappoint others.

The general had known several of the men present before he had assumed command of the Army of Arkansas and North Texas and all had served him well during the withdrawal. Through their efforts, it had been a planned retirement and not a rout followed by an undisciplined flight for safety. Having spent the past seven days in organizing their new defensive positions, he was taking the earliest possibility to warn them of the kind of conditions they would soon be facing.

"Well, gentlemen," Ole Devil said, in tones that carried to every corner of the room. "Firstly, I want to say—which will probably be a cause for relief to some of you—that I don't intend to make such gatherings a regular habit. We'll leave mass councils of war, complete with long, flowing bursts of oratory, to whoever is sent to replace General Culver."

There was a burst of laughter. Before his capture, General "Cussing" Culver had gained a name for frequently assembling every available officer—not merely those commanding regiments and companies or batteries—and indulging in long, verbose speeches as he explained his future policies.

"However," Ole Devil went on, when silence had returned, "I felt that, on this occasion, I should bring you all together and explain the situation. We have crossed the Ouachita and the work of consolidating our positions is well in hand. As most, if not all, of you have guessed, this is as far as we go."

A low rumble of satisfaction rose from the assembled officers. Looking at the rows of faces, Ole Devil saw no evidence of defeat or disillusionment despite the fact that they had withdrawn from the State's capital and left much of Arkansas in the Yankees' hands.

"How soon will we be taking the offensive, sir?" asked the tall, handsome, debonair Colonel Beauregard Gaylord; who had financed, recruited and trained his own cavalry regiment, Gaylord's Dare-Devils.

"We will not, at this time, be taking the offensive, gentlemen," Ole Devil warned.

"Will we after we've been reinforced, sir?" Colonel Harvey Barnett of the 1st Arkansas Rifle Regiment wanted to know.

"That's one of the things I wanted to explain," Ole Devil said soberly. "We aren't going to be reinforced. From now on, we will have to rely upon men recruited in Arkansas and Texas to keep our regiments up to strength."

"In that case, how can we hope to regain the land we've

given up," Barnett demanded, in a polite, respectful manner, and several of his regiment's officers muttered their agreement.

"We can't at this time," Ole Devil admitted, wishing that he could have given more reassuring news to the Arkansans—particularly those who had lived north of the Ouachita River. "As most of you know, the War isn't going too well for us. So it has been decided by the High Command that our main strength must be reserved for the protection of Richmond and the sea-board States. Without them, our cause is lost. From now on, they can't spare any further regiments, men, or much by way of military equipment."

"So we're to be left at the Yankees' mercy, sir?" suggested an Engineer's major bitterly, thinking of his home and business in Little Rock.

"Not entirely," Ole Devil corrected. "In fact, I'd say that we aren't at anybody's mercy. Rather we have been entrusted with a vital, important duty. From now on, gentlemen, we are to form a running sore in the Yankees' side. We have to make them expend men and material here that would otherwise be available for use in the East and South."

"How can we do that, sir?" inquired the tall, burly, bearded colonel who was the senior Artillery officer present and the commander of the Arkadelphia garrison. "We're still out-numbered and can't hope to face up to them in open battle."

"Our purpose isn't to try to beat them in open battle, Colonel Galveston," Ole Devil pointed out. "If it had been, we needn't have withdrawn from Little Rock. From now on, we concentrate upon holding our ground and fighting back, using the tactics of the Indians. And I mean using *all* their tactics, gentlemen, although we'll draw the line at some of their *methods*. Scalping isn't to be permitted." There were chuckles and he let them die down before continuing, "I realize that those of you who have the misfortune not to be Texans—" Again laughter rose and subsided. A general could always rely on such a response to his attempts at humour. Old Devil went on, "May not be sure just what fighting like Indians entails. It means that we will constantly be raiding the Yankees; striking at them when and where they least expect it; destroying their camps; running off their horses; wrecking and looting—especially the latter—their supply columns. Like the Indians, we will gather a good proportion of our military necessities from the Yankees. As you can see, it will mainly be work for the Cavalry. However, in addition to their work of patrolling the Ouachita and preventing the Yankees from crossing to raid us, the Infantry may be able to indulge in short distance raids beyond the river. The Artillery will be responsible, with Infantry support, for the protection of the riverside towns and villages. I can promise you, gentlemen, there will be work in plenty for everybody."

The words met with a mixed reception, especially amongst the more junior captains. Those in the Cavalry looked delighted at the prospect of such active, aggressive participation, with its accompanying opportunities for gaining distinction. Despite Ole Devil's promise of limited offensive action, the majority of the Infantry and all the Artillery officers—faced with what would most likely be considerable boredom in their defensive duties—seemed less pleased. However, one group who wore the blue facings of foot-soldiers did not appear to share their compatriots' gloom. They were members of the 2nd Texas Infantry Regiment, but were becoming a mounted force and, as such, would be able to operate with the Cavalry.

At the rear of the room, to the right of the big front doors of the building, sat Captain Dustine Edward Marsden Fog, youngest and most junior officer present. By his side was a taller, slightly older captain whose red facings indicated that he belonged to the Artillery. Dark-haired, moderately good looking, with a slim, wiry build, he was Douglas St. John Staunce, and he wore more formal, correct attire and accoutrements.

The only son of Britain's leading artillerist, Staunce had come from that country to command a battery of mountain howitzers in the Confederate States' Army. It had been presented to the South by a group of British cotton manufacturers and was manned by Crimean War veterans who had become disenchanted with civilian life. Staunce and his battery had also distinguished themselves at the Battle of Martin's Mill, but he had refused promotion as it would have meant that he must leave his men, battery and the four little guns.*

Since the Battle, Dusty and Staunce had frequently come into contact with each other. A close friendship had grown up between them, based on mutual admiration and respect. At the moment, however, neither spoke. They were listening to what was being said with considerable interest.

The abduction of General Culver had been completed without difficulty. Having accepted that defeat was inevitable, the Lancers' major had made certain that none of his men endangered their own—and their companions'— lives. Every time a soldier had appeared from the puptents, the major had called out and prevented him from doing anything rash. The Texans had taken away all the horses and had found the rest of their work just as easy. Escorting Culver and their loot to the Ouachita, they had made the crossing without meeting any opposition, then had delivered him to General Hardin's headquarters.

From the next morning, Dusty had been busy reorganizing his Company. Sufficient recruits had arrived from Texas for the men he had lost at Martin's Mill to be replaced and his command fetched up to its full strength. So he would rather have remained with them, helping to weld them and the old hands into a smoothly functioning team, but the meeting had taken precedence over that. The work had had to be left in the capable hands of 1st Lieutenant Blaze—for Red had matured rapidly while carrying out his first important independent assignment during the battle and, anyway, Dusty had always known he could be trusted to carry out his duties in a responsible manner—and Sergeant Major Billy Jack. Despite the latter's mournful,

---

* Traditionally, six guns formed a battery, but the Confederate States' Army's shortage of cannon rarely permitted them to achieve that number.

hang-dog aspect, he was a first-class soldier and stood high
in the enlisted men's esteem.

"I don't know who will take over command of the
Union's Army of Arkansas," Ole Devil admitted. "But,
until he gets here, there should be some confusion. I intend
that we should take full advantage of this and try to make it
worse. As the withdrawal proved, the Yankees aren't using
their top-quality regiments against us. With the exception
of the New Jersey Dragoons and, possibly, the Wisconsin
Heavy Infantry, we were and still are, opposed by me-
diocre outfits. That will make our work so much easier.
Such opposition will soon become disheartened, sullen and
discontented if they suffer constant harassment, misfortune
and danger. It's up to you, gentlemen, to make this state
happen."

"When Uncle Devil says 'you'," Dusty whispered to
Staunce. "He means *us*, the *cavalry*."

"That's family influence," the Englishman replied,
equally quietly. "Almost nepotism, old boy. Ole Devil's a
fly-slicer*, so one can expect him to be biased in favour.
Now if my father was commanding general, you'd really
see the Artillery in action."

"What can you wagon-soldiers† do that us leather
bumpers, or even the foot shufflers‡ can't do a heap better
and quieter?" Dusty challenged.

"Hit targets from farther away and harder than you can
with your revolvers and sabres," Staunce countered. "We
can stand back where you yellow-legs and the puddle-
splashers couldn't even—"

At that moment, Dusty's question received an even
more pointed answer.

There was a faint hissing sound, which rapidly grew
louder until it ended with a bellowing roar that shattered
the windows of the court house.

Every man in the room came to his feet and a thunder of

---

* Fly-slicers: derogatory name for cavalrymen.

† Wagon-soldiers: derogatory name for members of the field artillery.

‡Foot-shufflers: derogatory name for infantrymen.

startled conversation rolled forth. For a few seconds, everything was in confusion as officers turned to look in the direction of the explosion, or tried to leave their rows of seats to investigate.

Like the other occupants of the room, Dusty had risen. He found himself ideally positioned to take a hurried departure. Slapping on the hat he had been nursing, he darted forward and threw open the double doors. Before him stretched the town's square, and considerable pandemonium reigned across its width.

Civilians who had gathered before the court house, attracted by the presence of so many senior officers, scattered. Women were screaming and the men yelled incoherent warnings. About thirty yards away from the front entrance of the building was a fair-sized, smoking crater. As far as Dusty could see, nobody had been hurt in the explosion. However, all around the square, horses were rearing and plunging in fright. Cursing soldiers struggled to restrain the frightened animals and prevent them from bolting. Not all the attempts had been successful for some of the horses had escaped and were running away.

Looking around as he left the building, Dusty was grateful for his lack of seniority. Being by far the most junior officer present, he had had to leave his horse well away from the court house. So the high-spirited, big and powerful bay gelding appeared to be less disturbed than the animals which had been closer to the explosion.

Racing across the square, Dusty saw that Company "C's" guidon bearer had once more displayed competence in handling his duties. The good-looking, tall, sandy haired young private had already succeeded in bringing his own and Dusty's mounts under control.

Gripping one end of each horse's two-piece reins—the second portion being fastened to the saddle horn—Sandy McGraw had turned to face the court house. He watched the small Texan sprinting towards him. If he had been asked to bet on the subject, Sandy would have been willing to gamble heavily on his youthful officer being the first man to emerge from the building. What was more, the guidon bearer felt sure that Captain Fog was already assessing the situation and figuring out the best way to deal with it.

"What happened, Sandy?" Dusty called.

"Damned if I know, cap'n," the guidon bearer admitted, wishing that he could have made a more constructive or informative answer. "It just seemed to come from nowhere. I haven't even heard a cannon going off."

Neither had Dusty, which puzzled him.

Even before the withdrawal had commenced, Ole Devil had arranged for the riverside towns and villages to be defended. So there were well-protected and carefully sited batteries along the southern bank of the Ouachita, backed up by a strong force of infantry.

When the Yankees had arrived, they had brought three batteries of M1857 twelve-pounder "Napoleon" gun-howitzers. However, they had not been able to locate the weapons into a position from which they could bombard the town.

Aware of the danger presented by having so many senior officers gathered under one roof and in such close proximity to the enemy, Colonel Galveston had taken very strict security precautions. He had not been content to rely upon the secrecy with which the meeting had been arranged. Although the outskirts of Arkadelphia extended to the river, the court house was some distance from it. Neither the front of the building nor the square could be seen from the opposite side of the Ouachita. For all that, Colonel Galveston had given strict orders that a constant watch be kept on the Yankees and any sign of activity—particularly on the part of the "Napoleons"—must be reported to him immediately.

No such warning had been given. Nor could Dusty hear anything to suggest that the opposing forces were engaging each other with cannon-, or even rifle-fire. The lack of evidence of hostile activity was very puzzling.

If the Yankees had heard about the meeting and were hoping to kill a number of the Confederate senior officers, they would hardly have restricted their efforts to a single shot. Instead, they would have fired a volley from all eighteen of the three batteries' "Napoleons." To do that, however, they would have had to move into range and, by doing so, given the defenders some indication of their intentions.

"Dusty!" Staunce yelled, having reached the square shortly after the small Texan and discovered that his unattended horse had succeeded in freeing itself and bolting. "Where're you going?"

"To see what's happening from up on the hill," Dusty replied.

Among the precautions taken for the protection of Arkadelphia had been the establishment of an observation post on top of a nearby small hill. From it, the northern bank of the river could be kept under a more careful scrutiny than was possible at water-level. The men on duty had the use of a powerful telescope and could pass messages into town over a telegraph wire.

Dusty believed that, in the absence of sounds of conflict from alongside the river, the top of the hill would offer him the best opportunity of satisfying his curiosity.

"Loan me a horse and I'll come along," Staunce requested, glancing at the crater in passing. He had reached similar conclusions to Dusty's and felt that he was more capable of solving the mystery.

"Sure," Dusty agreed, without looking back. He was approaching his gelding and addressed the next words to the guidon bearer. "Let Captain Staunce borrow your horse, Sandy."

Grabbing the rein from the soldier's hand as he finished speaking, Dusty went astride the big bay with a flying bound. While his spurs' signal sent the animal bounding forward, with a powerful thrust of muscular energy that would have unseated a less able rider, he released the second strand of the reins and guided it in the required direction.

"Here, cap'n," Sandy said, passing his dun gelding's rein to Staunce. "I hope you can manage him."

"I'll try," the Englishman promised, gripping the low

horn of the double-girthed* Texas range saddle. "With all this leather weighing on his back, it shouldn't be too hard."

Swinging agilely abroad the dun, Staunce encouraged it to start moving. Sandy watched, expecting his spirited mount to display reluctance as it felt a stranger on its back. However, the horse could sense that it carried a rider capable of mastering it. So it responded to the instructions from Staunce's hands and heels, striding out after Dusty's fast-moving bay.

There was another hissing scream, followed by an explosion.

*Due to its Spanish connections, Texans rarely used the word "cinch."

CHAPTER FOUR

# Where the Hell's That Cannon?

Twisting on their saddles without reducing the horses' speed, the two young captains saw that a second crater had appeared about ten yards closer to the court house. The shell had fallen amongst the officers who were rushing from the building. Several of them were sprawling on the ground around the smoking hole. Some were starting to rise, but others lay writhing in agony and three remained motionless in growing pools of their blood.

As far as Dusty Fog could make out, none of his kinsmen, or anybody else belonging to the Texas Light Cavalry had been caught by the exploding shell. Relieved by that discovery, he turned to the front and urged his bay gelding to go even faster.

Although Staunce considered himself an expert horseman and had frequently ridden with some of Britain's best packs of foxhounds, he soon found that he had met his match in the small Texan. Lighter than the Englishman, sitting a larger, more powerful horse, Dusty continued to draw ahead and nothing Staunce could do served to lessen the distance between them. What was more, Staunce conceded that the same would most probably have happened even if they had been equal in size, weight and the quality of their mounts.

While for Staunce riding had only been a source of sport, or on occasion a way of getting from one place to another, a horse had always meant far more than that to Dusty and most other Texans. On the vast open ranges of the Lone Star State, a horse was a prime necessity of life. Without one, a man could not travel, work, or even survive for very long. So Texans tended to attain a greater profi-

ciency in equestrian matters than anything men in more
civilized areas needed to acquire.

There were three more explosions—at about one minute intervals—during the time taken by Dusty and Staunce
to climb the hill, warning them that the bombardment was
continuing. While they did not look back, the lack of noise
informed them that no exchange of fire had commenced
between the batteries facing each other across the river.

At the top of the hill, watched by half-a-dozen enlisted
men in Infantry uniforms, a worried-looking young second
lieutenant of the 1st Arkansas Rifles Regiment was peering
through a large telescope mounted on a tripod. Not far
away stood three wedge tents. The centre tent's front was
open, showing a civilian telegraphist seated at a table
which held his equipment. From it, a wire extended down
into the town.

Hearing the horses, the lieutenant raised his head. A
flicker of relief and recognition showed on his face.

"What's happening down there—Captain Fog?" the officer asked, remembering just in time that the small Texan
had been promoted for his part in the Battle of Martin's
Mill and being aware that recently appointed captains were
apt to be insistent on proper formalities when being addressed by their juniors in rank. "We keep hearing explosions."

"The Yankees are shelling the town," Dusty explained,
springing from the bay's back without waiting for it to
stop. He allowed it to go free and walked forward. "Can't
you see the gun that's doing it?"

"No," declared the lieutenant. "I've had a man watching
them all the time. Not one of their guns's manned, much
less being fired. All we've seen and heard are the explosions."

Another roar rang out from the town. Spinning around,
Dusty stared at the square. He could detect no sign of
where the shell had landed, but the figures outside the
court house were staring towards another building.

"Where'd that one hit?" Dusty wanted to know.

"I'm not sure," the lieutenant admitted, having started
to use the telescope once more. He swung it in an arc

before continuing, "I don't think they hit the court house this time."

Staunce arrived, bringing his borrowed mount to a rump-scraping halt near Dusty. Dismounting, the Englishman left the horse to fend for itself. Like the small Texan's bay, Sandy McGraw's dun did not stray far. After walking only a short distance, it came to a halt. Dusty's bay had already stopped and both animals stood ground-hitched by their trailing reins, as they had been trained to do.

"They've been hitting the court house, huh?" Dusty asked.

"They got it with their third and fourth shells," the lieutenant replied. "But they were too late. I saw General Hardin and most of the colonels leave by the side door before the shells started to hit. None of them'd been hurt 's I could make out."

"Where the hell's that cannon?" Staunce growled, glaring across the river.

"I can't see it anywhere," admitted the lieutenant, stepping aside and indicating the telescope. "Take a look for yourselves."

Striding forward fast, so as to beat Staunce and take the lieutenant's place, Dusty found that he could manipulate the instrument without needing to make adjustments to the tripod's height. Closing his left eye, he peered through the tube. First he looked at the square and court house. There were signs that some of the shells had penetrated the building. Windows which had escaped destruction in the first blasts had been shattered by detonations on the inside. Ole Devil, Colonel Mannen Blaze and other senior officers were gathered on the side of the court house farthest from the river. They were talking and staring towards the west side of the square.

Turning the telescope, Dusty lined it in the direction that his uncles were looking. A small knot of civilians had gathered about a crater outside a house. Nobody appeared to have been hurt. So Dusty swept his gaze over the Confederate defences. The batteries had been manned before the start of the meeting. Even as Dusty aimed at them, he saw his father—who looked like a taller, heavier and older version of himself—Major Hondo Fog, arrive and address the first lieutenant who was in temporary command of the positions.

Directing his attention across the river, Dusty studied the Yankees. They had set up camp beyond the range of the Confederate cannons and were preparing their positions. However, the guns' crews were not around their pieces. Instead, they stood in small groups near their quarters. Some of them were gazing at Arkadelphia, talking excitedly and pointing. Others had turned and were scanning the terrain behind them.

Dusty could see no suggestion of hostile activity being carried out, or even in preparation, among the Yankees. In fact, the impression he formed was that the shelling had been just as much of a surprise to them as it had been to its recipients. Satisfied that none of the "Napoleons" were in use, he searched for a hidden weapon in their vicinity. Yet, from the crews' reactions, he suspected that he would be wasting his time.

"Like you said," Dusty confirmed, at the conclusion of his scrutiny. "The shells aren't coming from the batteries across the Ouachita."

"That doesn't surprise me," Staunce declared. "They're being fired from something a damned sight heavier than any twelve-pounder 'Napoleon.' So the gun could be anywhere up to just over two miles from Arkadelphia. It's pretty far off, or we'd have heard it firing."

Accepting a more experienced man's assessment, particularly as it ran along similar lines to his own summation, Dusty decided to extend the area of his search. Before he could do so, another shell arrived in Arkadelphia. Altering the angle at which he had been looking, he found that it had plunged into a small house on the extreme eastern edge of the town. People were appearing from neighbouring buildings, converging rapidly on the stricken premises.

Cursing under his breath at such lousy shooting, Dusty elevated the telescope and gave greater attention to locating the mysterious weapon. He directed his search on either side of the trail that led from Arkadelphia—the river crossing having been made by ferry in times of peace—to Malvern, seat of Hot Spring County. The terrain was rolling, but open and offering few places suitable for concealing a large cannon. At last, however, about two miles beyond the river, the trail disappeared into a belt of woodland.

"I'm damned if I can see the son-of-a-bitching thing—," Dusty began, after a few seconds of searching along the horizon in response to a thought that had struck him.

"Then move over and let an expert find it," Staunce suggested, before the small Texan could continue with his explanation.

"Why sure," Dusty drawled, straightening up. "There's only the one, I'd say, or the shells'd be dropping a heap more frequently."

"Just the one," Staunce agreed, barely concealing his impatience to lay hands on the telescope. "But, if the craters and explosions were anything to go by, it's a big bastard."

"I started thinking it was real accurate, too," Dusty remarked, allowing his companion to have access to the instrument. "It only took three shots to hit the court house. I'd say that's tolerably good shooting."

"You don't know just *how* good," Staunce warned, duplicating Dusty's search of the river's edge; but for a different reason. "They must have somebody directing their fire for them."

"Likely," Dusty grunted non-committally.

"What I don't understand is why their 'Napoleons' aren't helping it out," the lieutenant put in. "They'd have been more likely to wipe out the meeting if they'd all cut loose at the same time."

"It's what I'd have expected to happen," Staunce admitted, without taking his eye from the telescope. "But the men at the batteries are acting as if they weren't expecting the shelling."

"I'd say that means the fellers with the big gun don't have their look-out with the Yankees on the river," Dusty remarked, watching the Englishman. "They couldn't've hid him and all the gear he'd need so's their own men wouldn't know he was there, even if there was any reason for them to do it."

"That's true enough," Staunce conceded, wondering if his companion was thinking on the right lines regarding the rest of the problem.

"So they've got him a whole heap closer to them," Dusty suggested.

"Where do you think he might be?" Staunce challenged.

"Somewhere high enough to see where the shells are falling—"

"Which narrows the field of search a little. He'll have to be on top of a piece of high ground—"

"Or well *above* it," Dusty interrupted quietly.

"*Above* it?" the Englishman repeated.

"*Well* above it," Dusty corrected, delighted to discover that his companion had failed to duplicate his findings.

"A balloon!" Staunce breathed. Although he had considered the possibility, he had discarded it as being most unlikely. Returning his attention to the telescope, he scanned above the sky-line and soon detected a small round blob hanging almost motionless above the trees. "You tricky blighter, Dusty! You'd already figured out what was happening and why."

"All of us fly-slicers're mighty slick," Dusty commented in tones redolent of false modesty. "They had to be watching from somewhere—"

"I haven't seen any balloon!" protested the lieutenant, displaying alarm at what he suspected might be called an error on his part.

"It's there, mister," Staunce declared. "I'd say close to five hundred feet above the woods on the right of the Malvern trail."

"Damn it!" the lieutenant ejaculated. "How was I to know? My orders were to keep watch on the Yankees' positions along the river, not to—"

"Like you said, mister," Dusty put in. "How were you

to know? Nobody could have guessed that they'd make this kind of play. Can you see the gun, Doug?"

"I'm damned if I can," Staunce replied, after carrying out another careful examination of the woodland in the vicinity of the balloon. "But they must be fairly close, so the observer can pass down his corrections either by shouting, dropping notes, or through a telegraph wire. Even if he's using telegraph, they're not likely to be too far apart."

"There's wooded country on both sides of the trail," Dusty pointed out. "I've heard that one of those balloons needs a fair amount of heavy, bulky gear to get into the air and I couldn't see any of it. So I reckon it and the cannon're hidden among the trees. Not too far from the trail, either. A gun that big'll take a heap of moving and won't be so easy to man-handle as one of your lil ole howitzers."

"That's true," Staunce confirmed, concentrating his scrutiny on the distant woodland. "But I can't see any—".

There was another explosion in the town. Although Dusty and Staunce had not seen it, the enlisted men were looking down.

"Hell's fire!" yelled the corporal who was present. "They're aiming for the houses, not our guns!"

Turning his gaze to Arkadelphia, Dusty saw people running to a store. Its front had been blown in by the shell.

"Why the hell don't our guns start shooting back?" raged a private and the other enlisted men spluttered furious agreement.

Turning his eyes towards the defensive batteries, Dusty saw—although his ears had already informed him—that they were still inactive. A moment's thought gave him the reason for their refusal to open fire.

"Even if they could see the gun that's doing the shelling," the small Texan explained, "they couldn't reach it. And if they start throwing lead across the river, the Yankees're sure to cut loose back at them. Which'll get the town damaged a whole heap worse than with one gun shooting."

In view of Dusty's youth and small size, the infantrymen might have disregarded his comments as unworthy of

their attention. However, they had identified him and knew
of his part in the Battle of Martin's Mill and also as the
captor of General Culver. So they figured that anything he
said was likely to have merit and be worth listening to.
Once the basic facts had been pointed out and elaborated
upon, they could see the wisdom of their batteries refrain-
ing from opening fire.

"Hey!" yelled one of the enlisted men, pointing downwards. "There's a Yankee going like a bat out of hell along
the Malvern trail."

"Likely he's headed for the gun," Dusty guessed. "What
do you make of him, Doug?"

"A lieutenant," Staunce answered, having adjusted the
telescope's alignment. "Artilleryman, going by his red
sash. Riding fast."

"Hey, you fellers!" called the telegraph operator—who,
being a civilian and employed by a private company instead of the Army, as was the policy in the Confederate
States, had no need to conform with military courtesy—
looking out of his wedge-tent. "There's a message just
come through from Colonel Galveston. He wants to know
why the hell we haven't reported the shooting."

"What shall I tell him?" asked the lieutenant, looking
worriedly from one captain to the other.

"You might say that you thought he knew it was happening," Staunce suggested, "but I don't think that it
would be very well received."

"Try telling him there's no sign of activity along the
river," Dusty advised, seeing the alarm on the lieutenant's
face and taking pity on him. "Then say the shelling's being
done by one big gun that's hidden in the woods about two
miles away and close to the Malvern trail. Say you haven't
been able to locate the gun's exact position, but it's got a
balloon observing for it. I reckon you and I'd best go down
and report, Doug."

"It would be the polite thing to do," Staunce admitted,
leaving the telescope and looking at the lieutenant. "While
you're at it, you'd better ask the colonel if he wants you to

keep watching the Yankees' positions or to try to find exactly where the big gun is."

"I'll do that, sir," the lieutenant promised. "I might locate it by watching that officer who rode out."

"I was just going to suggest that," Dusty remarked with a grin, watching the lieutenant—whose face showed relief at having been given the answer to his problem—scuttling away towards the telegraphist's tent.

"And me," admitted the Englishman. "I'm pleased that he thought of it himself."

"Won't old Galveston be pot-boiling mad, though?" Dusty drawled.

"That's *very* likely," Staunce smiled. "And he'll be looking for somebody to lay the blame on. So we'd better get down there, or he may decide that we'll do for it."

Collecting their horses, Dusty and Staunce mounted. Despite the Englishman's comment and an awareness of the situation's gravity, they intended to return to Arkadelphia at a more leisurely pace than they had used when ascending the hill. The telegraph would have relayed their discoveries and conclusions long before they could hope to have done so themselves, no matter how hard they had pushed their mounts. Having no wish to punish their horses unnecessarily, they held their pace to a fast walk.

"I wonder what that blighter's up to, Dusty?" Staunce said, pointing to where the Union officer was galloping along the Malvern trail.

"Likely going to tell them to get their aim straight and start hitting our batteries," the small Texan suggested, watching a shell explode in the centre of a street far from the river.

"They don't seem to be ranging in very well," the Englishman admitted. "I would have expected them to be on to their targets by now."

"They didn't waste too many shells in hitting the court house," Dusty drawled. "Just two, getting closer each time, then in through the roof."

"You don't think they're just shelling the town indiscriminately, do you?" Staunce asked, for such an idea had never occurred to him.

"I'd hate like hell to think that even a Yankee soft-shell*
would do *that*," Dusty answered. "What kind of gun do
you reckon it is, Doug?"

"A twenty-four-, or maybe even a thirty-pounder
'rifle,'" Staunce replied.

"As big's that, huh?" Dusty breathed, knowing the word
"rifle" used in such a fashion meant a cannon with a rifled
barrel.

"At least that big," Staunce confirmed. "A twelve-, or
even an eighteen-pounder couldn't be throwing from anywhere near that balloon and wouldn't have made such big
craters. And a smooth-bore couldn't pitch its balls accurately."

Once again, Dusty followed his companion's meaning
without the need for further explanation. In the period of
his training at Judge Blaze's small military academy—in
Polveroso City, Rio Hondo County, Texas—Dusty's educa-
tion had covered many aspects of Army life. Although he
had been intended to join the Texas Light Cavalry, he was
encouraged to study training Manuals devoted to Infantry
and Artillery matters. From his reading, he knew that the
spin imparted to a shell by the grooves of a "rifle's" barrel
enabled it to fly more accurately than a round shot from a
smooth-bore cannon. He also had a fair idea of a thirty-
pounder's dimensions.

"Happen you're right," Dusty said, trying to sound as if
he doubted that such an unlikely thing could happen. "It'll
be a fair-sized hunk of iron to haul around."

"If it's a Parrot thirty-pounder rifle, which I'm inclined
to believe it is, it will have a tube over eleven feet long.
With the carriage and limber, it weighs almost nine thousand pounds."

"You'd need ten, maybe even a dozen *big* horses to pull
it," Dusty said, after Staunce's description, speaking half
to himself. "And they won't be moving anywhere near as
fast as a flying artillery battery†."

* Soft-shell: a liberal-intellectual of the most bigoted kind.

† Flying artillery: light field, or horse, artillery capable of operating
with the cavalry.

"They're not meant to," Staunce pointed out. "They're siege, or even garrison pieces, not field guns. What's on your mind, Dusty?"

"Somebody's going to have to do something about that blasted big gun," the small Texan replied.

# CHAPTER FIVE

## Somebody's Come Across the River

"Let's hope there's a cup of coffee, even if we can't get a meal at Stilton Crossing," Captain Dusty Fog remarked to Captain Douglas St. John Staunce as they rode slowly through the darkness. "It'll be way too late for any by the time we reach Camden."

Holding their horses to a steady walk—Staunce having retrieved his from the party of 2nd Texas Infantry who had been catching the animals that had bolted when the first shell exploded—the two young officers were traversing the trail that ran parallel with the southern bank of the Ouachita River. They were going to Camden, seat of Ouachita County, to rejoin their commands after the conclusion of the meeting in Arkadelphia. Dusty's guidon bearer, Sandy McGraw, had been sent ahead with dispatches from Colonel Mannen Blaze to the headquarters of the Texas Light Cavalry. All the other officers would be following the next day.

As the pair did not expect to reach their destination much before midnight, they were hoping to obtain refreshment at the part of the river known as Stilton Crossing. Several civilian workers had been hired to establish positions from which two batteries of "Napoleons"—the Model of 1857 gun-howitzer was the workhorse of both armies' Artillery—could help to prevent the Yankees from making attempts at utilizing the easy crossing at that point. A small detachment of the Texas Light Cavalry had been assigned to guard the workers. Their officer would be willing to trade cups of coffee and, possibly, food for news of the gathering attended by his visitors.

"I wonder if the patrol's managed to get at that big

51

gun?" Dusty went on after a few seconds' silence, repeating a subject that had cropped up on two previous occasions.

"They ought to be getting close to it, even if it pulled out after the crew stopped shelling Arkadelphia," Staunce replied, looking at the small figure by his side. "You would have liked to go after it yourself, wouldn't you?"

"Sure I would," Dusty replied, grimly and bitterly, thinking of the scenes he had witnessed during the return from the observation post on the hill. There had been dead and wounded civilians among the burning, shell-damaged buildings of what had been a peaceable, pleasant little town. "The bastards must have been shooting deliberately, meaning to kill civilians."

"It seemed that way," the Englishman conceded, in tones which matched his companion's. "What a lousy way to make war."

"Lousy's too mild a word for it," Dusty declared. "Whoever ordered it done deserves to be hanged."

"Did you ask if you could go after the gun?"

"I didn't need to. Uncle Devil and Uncle Mannen knew what was on my mind as soon as they saw me."

"And gave you good reasons why you couldn't handle it," Staunce pointed out, knowing his young companion wished to talk as a means of getting the anger and disgust he had been feeling out of his system.

"Sure," Dusty agreed. "Arkadelphia's part of the Texas Mounted Infantry's bailiwick. So it was up to them to take on the chore."

"That was true enough," Staunce stated. "You wouldn't have liked it if another cavalry regiment had been assigned to work in your area."

"Likely," Dusty sighed. "They were the nearest outfit of horse soldiers, even if they've only just taken on the name 'Mounted.'"

"And it would have taken two days at the least to fetch Company 'C' up the Camden."

"I'm not gainsaying that."

"Don't you think the Mounted Infantry can handle it?" Staunce challenged.

"There's no reason why they can't," Dusty admitted.
"Most of them hail from North Texas, but they've all done
plenty of riding and know how to fight on the back of a
horse. It's just—Well. I saw what that damned big gun had
done to the town and I was madder than a boiled owl."

"We all were," Staunce said. "But we couldn't all go. If
we had, it would have meant a full-scale confrontation with
the Yankees. And that's one thing we can't chance right
now."

"Are you trying to convince me, or yourself?" Dusty
inquired.

"I wish I knew," Staunce answered, then partially
changed the subject to something which had been puzzling
him. "Why do you think they stopped the bombardment
soon after that lieutenant reached them?"

"Could be that's what he'd been sent to tell them to do,"
Dusty guessed. "There aren't many Yankee officers who'd
condone, or allow, the indiscriminate shelling of civilian
property."

"You could be right—" the Englishman began.

Any further comment Staunce may have considered
making was forgotten. The trail passed through fairly thick
woodland, with a heavy coating of bushes on either side.
There was little light filtering down from the stars and half
moon, but the two captains' eyes had grown accustomed to
the gloom. They could make out the shapes of their horses
and see a short way ahead.

Suddenly Dusty's big bay gelding snorted, threw up its
head, pricked its ears and stared towards the bushes on the
right side of the trail.

There was a rustling commotion amongst the undergrowth. Something fairly large lunged into view, bounding
in front of the riders. Controlling their startled mounts with
deft ease, the officers reached rapidly towards their
weapons. While Staunce's right hand was still trying to
free the flap of his close-topped official issue holster—and
he had trained himself to be far from slow at this—Dusty's
left fist had stabbed across, drawn and cocked the off side
white-handled Army Colt. Despite having aligned the barrel on the swiftly moving shape and holding back the trig-

ger with his forefinger, Dusty did not complete the draw by releasing the hammer.

Sailing back into the air, with the kind of leap for which its species was famous, a large buck whitetail deer passed across the trail in front of Dusty and Staunce. It disappeared, to alight in the bushes on the river's side of the path and continued its flight. When it landed the second time, there was a hollow, wooden thumping noise far different from how its previous return to the ground had sounded.

"If you'd have been faster, we could have had venison for dinner tomorrow," the Englishman complained, closing the holster's flap. "What's wrong?"

Having returned the Colt to leather, with a spinning twirl on his trigger-finger as a preliminary, Dusty was swinging from his saddle.

"I'm going to see what he landed on the second time," the small Texan replied, dropping his reins.

"It did sound a trifle odd," Staunce conceded, also dismounting. "I'll come with you."

Advancing cautiously into the undergrowth, they spread out and moved in the direction which had been taken by the fleeing buck. A startled, or chased, whitetail deer could cover up to twenty feet in a single leap. So Dusty and Staunce were approaching the bank of the river before the mysterious sound was explained. A small boat had been turned upside down and was concealed amongst the bushes. Dusty found it and, placing his left hand on the keel, felt at the wood.

"It's still wet, Doug," the small Texan said, having called his companion over and announced his discovery. "Somebody's come across the river."

"It could have been a family, or a man, who wanted to get away from the Yankees," Staunce suggested.

"Why sure," Dusty drawled, bending to grip the side of the boat and turn it the right way up. "Only, if it had been, I don't reckon they'd've bothered to hide it like this."

"There's something under it," Staunce remarked, feeling into his trouser pocket. He produced a box of Phosphorus "Strike-Anywhere" matches and lit one.

In the sudden glow of light, ignoring the anything but pleasant smell that always accompanied the ignition of a phosphorus match, the captains looked at a small, oblong, tarpaulin-wrapped bundle. Dusty drew the Russell-Barlow folding knife which his Cousin, Red Blaze had given to him as a replacement for one lost during the Battle of Martin's Mill, and used it to open the wrappings. Any lingering notions either of them might have harboured about the boat having carried refugees to safety were brought to an end in no uncertain way.

Setting off another match, before the first had burned itself out, Staunce joined Dusty in staring at the printed words on the top sheet of the papers that had been exposed by the removal of the tarpaulin.

### *"PEOPLE OF THE OUACHITA RIVER TAKE WARNING*

> *General A. G. Culver was abducted by members of the Rebel Army. Unless he is released, we will be compelled to destroy your homes. This is no idle threat. We have already bombarded the town of Arkadelphia and will continue with our attacks until General Culver is liberated."*

Staunce had become so engrossed that he allowed the match to burn down to his fingers. With a startled curse, he shook it out and flung it aside.

"It *was* a deliberate bombardment!" the Englishman ejaculated.

"Yes," Dusty replied quietly. "I didn't think Culver's men thought so highly of him."

"Or me," Staunce admitted, then his anger got the better of him. "Damn it all, Dusty. This is barbaric."

"There's no nice way of fighting a war," Dusty pointed out.

"I know that. But there are certain things one doesn't do."

"Likely. What shall we do about this, Doug?"

"Burn it and the boat," Staunce declared, tapping the bundle of paper. "We don't want any civilians to see what's printed here."

"That's for sure," Dusty drawled. "But there's the feller who fetched them from across the river for us to think about. We'll need to nail his hide to the wall, if it can be done."

"It *can* be, I'd say," Staunce answered. "He'll have to come back for his bundle. So all we have to do is wait in hiding and grab him."

"Tonight?"

"Don't you think he'll come back?"

"Not tonight," Dusty guessed. "If he'd wanted them for tonight, he'd've taken them with him."

"Possibly," Staunce admitted. "Do you think he came from Camden?"

"Maybe. Or he could've come up from Vaden, except we should've met him on the trail."

"Unless he hid when he saw or heard us coming."

"It's possible," Dusty drawled. "You're the senior of us, Doug, but—was it me—I'd say take the papers with us to Stilton Crossing. The feller might've come from there. It'd be a damned sight more handy for one of the workers than a jasper out of Camden, or Vaden."

"That's what I was going to suggest, not being one for pulling rank," the Englishman smiled. "We might be able to arrange for the guard at the crossing to have somebody keep watch over the boat."

Returning to the horses, after Dusty had rewrapped the parcel, they mounted and continued with their interrupted journey. As they rode, they talked about their find; but without reaching any definite conclusions.

About another mile fell behind them before they saw the lights of the construction camp. There was little activity among the small cluster of buildings of the hamlet, or around the tents in which the workers and guards were housed. A Texas Light Cavalry sentry challenged them, from a place of concealment amongst a clump of bushes. On identifying themselves, he allowed them to pass through.

"Who's the guard's officer?" Dusty inquired.

"Mr. Clements," replied the sentry, pointing. "You'll find him in the wall-tent down by the houses."

"I thought all you Texas Light Cavalry officers were called 'Hardin,' 'Blaze,' or 'Fog,'" Staunce remarked, as he and Dusty turned their horses in the direction indicated by the soldier.

"It's all lies, started by folks who aren't called 'Hardin,' 'Blaze,' or 'Fog,'" the small Texan explained. "We've got a Major Smith."

"*Smith!*" the Englishman repeated. "I don't believe it."

"It's true," Dusty insisted, straight-faced. "He married my Aunt Cecilia Blaze and we couldn't get him to take *her* name."

"That figures," Staunce sighed, then gave an exasperated cluck. "Damn it, I'm starting to talk like you foreigners now."

"Why thank you, 'most to death." Dusty drawled. "It's good of you to say so."

"At least Lieutenant Clements isn't a Hardin, Fog or Blaze," Staunce said, in tones of relief. "That's something."

By that time, they had reached the wall-tent. Its door flaps were open and the interior was illuminated by a lamp. As the two captains rode up, a tall, wide-shouldered first lieutenant in his middle-twenties emerged.

"Howdy, Cousin Dusty," the lieutenant greeted.

"I might have known!" Staunce groaned.

"Howdy, Cousin Shad," Dusty acknowledged, ignoring his companion's comment. "Do you know Captain Staunce?"

"I've heard tell of you, Captain," Shadrack Clements declared. "Coffee's hot, happen you feel like stopping a spell and taking a cup."

"That's one of the reasons we dropped by, Shad," Dusty informed his cousin, swinging from his saddle and looking at the wedge-tents which housed the guard and workers. "Kind of quiet tonight."

"That's the way I like it," Clements replied. "I hope your meeting went the same way."

"There's some might've called it that," Dusty said quietly and his cousin shot a glance his way. "I'll tell you about it inside, Shad."

Having dismounted, the two captains left their horses ground hitched and followed Clements into the officer of the guard's quarters. Although the structure had a triangular top like the two-men pup- and four-men wedge-tents, its twenty-four inches high perpendicular walls—from which its name derived, gave it a greater height and size. In spite of the short time that the camp had been erected, the officer's wall-tent offered a fair standard of comfort. It had a small stove at the rear, on which a pot of coffee was bubbling. A collapsible table, two chairs, a small chest-of-drawers, a bed and a wash-stand completed the furnishings.

"Some of the good ladies back to Camden asked if they could fix it up a mite," Clements explained, seeing Staunce was studying the interior. "Rest your feet a spell, while I fetch on the coffee."

Taking the chairs, Dusty and the Englishman waited for their host to produce and fill cups with coffee. When that was done, Dusty told his cousin what had happened in Arkadelphia. Clements growled out a curse as he heard of the shelling, then cast another glance at the tarpaulin-covered package which Staunce had brought in and placed on the table.

"How're you getting on with the civilian workers, Shad?" Dusty inquired, at the completion of his story.

"Most of them're all right," Clements replied. "Fact being, apart from the one called Fletcher, they're all decent enough fellers for goober-grabbers."*

"You know them pretty well then?" Dusty went on.

"Not socially, or anything like that, but I figured it'd be best to at least get to know their names and something about them."

"Where're they at now?" Staunce wanted to know.

"Gone into town, like every night," the lieutenant replied, alternating puzzled looks between his visitors.

* Goober-grabber: a native of Arkansas.

"None of them live in Camden, but they go to the Tavern. It's a heap more fun than staying out here. Comes midnight, most of them'll be rolling back—and do I mean rolling, some of them anyways. Maybe you'd best tell me what's on your minds."

"I reckon that would be best," Dusty agreed, knowing Clements to be a shrewd man, and did as requested.

"You figure the horned toad who fetched these over the river's come from here?" Clements demanded, after Dusty had finished speaking, looking at a notice that Staunce had taken from the package.

"He could be," Dusty answered. "It's more likely to be from here than out of Camden, or Vaden."

"I'll float my stick with you on that," Clements conceded. "Just one, or more of them?"

"One man *could* have handled the boat, even to hauling it out, turning it over and hiding it," Dusty replied. "Comes morning, happen you've got somebody who can read sign, you could have him go and see what he thinks; although we've probably walked where we shouldn't have."

"I'll do that," Clements promised. "If it is one of them, I reckon it'll be best if he's caught."

"That's for sure," Dusty drawled. "And the sooner the better."

"The difficult thing will be catching him," Staunce pointed out.

"I was just thinking that same thing," Dusty admitted. "But one thing I'm sure of. We're going to find out who he is."

## CHAPTER SIX

# Hang a Couple of Them!

Standing near one of the holes being dug as emplacements from which the 12-pounder "Napoleon" gun-howitzers could help to defend Stilton Crossing, Captain Dusty Fog overtly studied the nine civilian workmen as they climbed out at the conclusion of their day's work. Most of them had bruised faces, or showed other signs of having been involved in a fight. However, Dusty was less interested in that than in detecting any suggestion of them knowing him. If they did, some of them might be aware that all was not as it should be in the light of recent events.

It was almost sundown on the day after Dusty's discovery of the boat and the printed threat, apparently from the United States' Army of Arkansas, to the people who lived along the southern bank of the Ouachita River. Dusty had just returned to Stilton Crossing, accompanied by twelve carefully selected members of Company "C." On their arrival, they had relieved the other soldiers of the Texas Light Cavalry who had performed the guard duty during the previous evening.

Having already started to think how it might be possible to trap the traitor, if he should be at the camp, Dusty had insisted that he and Captain Staunce should leave before the civilian workers returned from visiting Camden. Going to the town and taking rooms in the best hotel, the captains had contrived to avoid being seen by the workmen and had awaited developments.

One of Lieutenant Clements' soldiers had possessed the necessary ability to read tracks. At dawn, as soon as there had been sufficient light, he had been sent to carry out an examination of the area around Dusty's find. On his return, he had declared that he had found evidence to suggest that only one man had drawn the boat from the water, then passed through the bushes on to the Arkadelphia-Camden trail. The nature of the terrain had precluded any hopes of obtaining clues to the mysterious person's identity. Due to the hard ground underfoot and the walker having had to force his way through the undergrowth, the soldier could not even establish his height or weight from the length and depth of his stride. However, he had gone from the boat to the trail at an angle that had suggested he was making for Camden—or Stilton Crossing.

Clements had reported his man's findings to the two captains. In addition, the lieutenant had announced that he had checked up on his guard detail and was satisfied that none of them could have left the camp, crossed the Ouachita and returned with the bundle of warning notices. Wishing to avoid arousing suspicion, he had not questioned the civilians.

Having arranged for his cousin to keep a careful, if surreptitious, watch on the suspects, Dusty had accompanied Staunce to the headquarters of the Texas Light Cavalry. They had informed Major Smith, who was in command until the return of the other senior officers, of their discovery and plans. Giving his official sanction, the major had left the affair in their hands. To ensure its success, they had been compelled to cause a lot of work for a considerable number of people. Dusty hoped that the effort expended would be justified by the final results.

If Dusty was studying the civilians, they in turn were subjecting him to a more obvious scrutiny. He waited to catch some comment which would suggest that one, or more, of them knew something was wrong with his appearance. For his part in the scheme, he had reverted to wearing the official type of uniform that the late Captain von Hertz had insisted upon him adopting; even down to the waist belt and a first lieutenant's insignias of rank. It was a much less impressive outfit than the skirtless tunic and the Western gun-rig.

"Look at the short-grown bastard!" muttered the middle-sized, lean and bitter-faced man called Fletcher, scowling in Dusty's direction and apparently neither knowing, or caring, that his words were reaching the young officer's ears. He alone of the civilians bore no evidence of having been fighting the night before. "Trust a lousy dressed-up button like him to just stand there watching folks work."

"He's doing his share by fighting the War," protested the big, burly, jovial-featured Amos Meats tolerantly.

"That ain't likely," Fletcher answered. "He don't look dry behind the ears, much less been doing any fighting."

"Even if he's not done any yet," Meats countered, "he'll likely be doing it soon. And anybody who's willing to fight them Yankee bastards's all right with me."

"He *may* get 'round to fighting 'em," Fletcher grumbled. "But it's poor bastards like us who have to do all the sweating and work."

"I don't mind how much hard work I do," Meats stated, a touch pompously, "just so long as it helps to lick those Goddamned Yankees."

"Ole Amos sure hates Yankees," chortled one of the other men.

"I'd kill every last son-of-a-bitching one of 'em, was I given the chance," Meats declared, scowling with the kind of patriotic fervour his companions had come to know and expect. "And until the chance comes my way, I'm willing to do a bit of work. You should be too, Fletch."

There was a mumble of good-natured agreement from the rest of the civilians. While Fletcher had taken the job rather than accept an offer to enlist in Confederate States' Army and was receiving a higher rate of pay than the soldiers, he never stopped complaining about the work, food, accommodation, or conditions in general. He appeared to begrudge every effort he was called upon to make for the Southron cause.

On the other hand, Meats was invariably cheerful, hard working and fanatically devoted to the Confederate States. Almost embarrassingly so, his companions considered. Last night, at the Tavern, a group of Camden citizens had been criticizing Ole Devil Hardin's conduct of the War. They had become most indignant when Meats had intervened. As a result, there had been a fight which had seen three of their number put in the hospital. The rest had, however, avoided being jailed for their part in the brawl by Meats making the town's constable realize the importance of their work.

Watching and listening to the men, Dusty turned over in his mind all the information his cousin had been able to give to him. Clements had studied the civilians since his arrival and had drawn conclusions which Dusty believed would be objective and close to correct. However, the lieutenant had been inclined to believe that—if there was a traitor in the camp—Fletcher was the most likely suspect. Dusty preferred to keep an open mind on the subject and to await developments. Unless he was mistaken, they should soon be starting to happen.

And they did!

"Look!" screeched one of the civilians, dropping his pick as he stared and pointed towards the near-by woodland.

Figures were rushing from among the trees. Carrying Springfield carbines, they wore the uniforms of the United States' Cavalry.

Letting out a startled yell, Dusty grabbed for and began to fumble with the flap of his holster. He did not display any of his usual skill in handling the awkward rig.

Firing as they approached, with their weapons belching clouds of white powder smoke, the attackers scored hits and at least one near miss. Dirt flew between Dusty's spread apart feet as a bullet churned into the ground. Having turned and started to raise his Enfield carbine, Sandy McGraw screamed. He spun around, throwing aside the weapon, and sprawled face down. The other three men on duty also went down, although in a less spectacular manner.

Bursting out of the wedge tents, the rest of the guard showed that they had been caught unawares by the attack. One of them tried to draw a revolver, but was fired on by the Yankee sergeant—a tall, lean man whose hawk-nosed, high cheekboned, savage dark features might have implied mixed Indian and white blood. Crying in agony, the stricken soldier twirled and tumbled back into the tent.

At the shooting of the man by his side, the short, white-haired and ancient-looking Corporal Hassle elevated his hands. It was an example followed by the remainder of the soldiers.

"Don't shoot, blast ye!" the old non-com howled. "We've quit. It ain't no use doing nothing else."

"How about you, luff?"* demanded the tall, lean, Union captain, his voice holding a hard Teutonic timbre, as some of his men trained their weapons in Dusty's direction.

"All right," the small Texan agreed, sounding what he hoped would be angry and frightened. He thrust his hands hurriedly into the air, yelping, "All *right!* I surrender."

While speaking, Dusty darted a glance in the civilians' direction. He could see alarm on their faces, but nothing to suggest that any of them doubted the authenticity of the "attack." Not that he felt too surprised at their acceptance of the situation. If he had not been aware of their "assailants'" identities, he might have taken them for genuine Yankees.

Captain Staunce and the selected members of Company "C" looked every inch of hard-bitten, hard-travelled Union cavalrymen. Having been aware that the need for such disguises might arise, once the withdrawal had been halted on the south shore of the Ouachita River, Ole Devil and Colonel Blaze had caused perfect copies of Federal uniforms and equipment to be made and held at the Texas Light Cavalry's headquarters.

To be truthful, a certain amount of luck was helping the deception. Shortly after Dusty's arrival at the regiment, Red Blaze had returned with the Company from an all-night training exercise. So the small Texan had told the men he had selected to become "Yankees" neither to wash nor shave. Staunce had already omitted his morning ablutions, complaining bitterly and half seriously about the results of such behaviour. To augment their appearances of having ridden long, fast, and hard, they had immersed themselves in the river and their clothing bore evidence of the fact.

* Luff: derogatory name for a first lieutenant.

Moving forward, the "Yankees" acted as they might have been expected to under the circumstances. Some went to watch over the "surrendered" Texans. Others gathered around the civilians, or went to examine the "shot" soldiers. Two of them took hold of and dragged away Sandy McGraw's "body." He had been the "victim" nearest to the workmen and the most likely for them to have discovered was not really dead or injured. Accompanied by his sergeant—who now bore the same rank in Company "C" and went by the name Kiowa Cotton—and "Private" Red Blaze, Staunce approached Dusty.

"All right, luff," Staunce said harshly. "I want to know where your outfit is, how many men're in it and what you're going to be doing in the future."

"I won't tell you!" Dusty declared.

"Like hell you won't!" Red growled, hiding the delight he was feeling at the part he now had to play.

With that, the red-head took his left hand from the foregrip of the Springfield carbine. The weapon, like the rest carried by the impostors, was a battle field "purchase." Up swung Red's left arm, driving the back of his hand against the side of Dusty's face. Red had been told to make the blow look natural and he threw himself into it with his usual gusto. Nobody, particularly its recipient, could have doubted that the red-head's attack was genuine. Spun on his heels by the impact, Dusty crashed to the ground.

"That won't help!" Staunce barked as Red advanced and drew back a foot as if meaning to kick his cousin. "Leave him to me. On your feet, *luff*."

Slowly, shaking his head and rubbing at his reddened, stinging cheek, Dusty obeyed. He faced the three "Yankees," trying to look defiant and avoiding turning his eyes to the men for whom the whole performance was being carried out. For all that, he knew that he and his companions were holding the civilians' attention. He hoped that they were being convinced—and that one of them really was the traitor.

"I asked you a question, luff," Staunce continued, glowering at the small Texan and retaining his Teutonic accent. "I want to know where your outfit is, how many men are in it, and what your future orders might be."

"Do what you like to me," Dusty challenged, in what he believed to be the correct tone of voice. "You'll never make me answer."

"Want to bet on it?" Red inquired, making as if to attack again.

"That's enough!" Staunce snarled, for the red-head was not such a good mimic and his Texas drawl was noticeable. A glance suggested to the captain that it had gone unnoticed. "Keep your damned mouth shut, Broski. And you, luff, this is your last chance to answer."

"I'm in the 11th Kentucky Heavy Infantry," Dusty replied hastily. "We're fifteen hundred strong—"

"And you're a liar!" Staunce interrupted. "Maybe you think I'm playing games. I'll show you." He looked at the group by the wedge-tents. "Hey, you with those peckerwood bastards. Hang a couple of them!"

Startled exclamations rose from the civilians. However, their guards threatened them with the carbines. So they restricted their objections to speech and not action. The Springfield was a single-shot weapon, but not all of the "Yankees" had used their solitary loads when capturing the camp. There was no way for the civilians to know which of the muzzles directed at them was still capable of throwing out flame, smoke and lead.

Being unable to put up any resistance, the workmen watched six of the "Yankees" hustling Corporal Hassle and another small enlisted man towards the trees. The rest of the "prisoners'" guards continued to watch over their "captives," for Dusty had warned them that they must do nothing that might warn the civilian of the situation's true nature.

Taking their two "victims" to the edge of the woods, the "Yankees" brought up a pair of horses. While Hassle's and the private's arms were being bound to their sides, ropes were tossed over the branches of a big oak tree in plain view of the civilians. Struggling futilely, the "victims" were hoisted on to the McClellan saddles. Dusty had insisted that this type of rig be used, in case the man he was hoping to locate should be suspicious, alert for traps and sufficiently observant to notice apparently minor details. With the two men mounted, nooses were dropped about their necks and tightened.

"This's murder!" Dusty croaked, watching the civilians.

Although every one of them looked alarmed, it was nothing more as yet.

Two hands rose and fell, slapping the horses' rumps. Bounding forward, the animals left their burdens dangling with wildly kicking legs from the limbs of the tree. Horrified gasps and disgusted exclamations burst from the civilians. To Dusty, it seemed that Fletcher and Meats reacted somewhat more slowly than the rest of their party. For all that, both of them seemed to be visibly shaken by what they had seen.

"Well," Staunce said to Dusty. "Are you ready to tell me the truth?"

"No!" the small Texan replied.

"I'll hang every one of your men, unless you tell me."

"Then do it. They're soldiers and will have to take their chances."

"Like you said," Staunce growled. *"They're* soldiers and have to take their chances. So I'll start to hang the civilians."

"The *civilians?"* Dusty repeated, in tones of horror and there was a louder rumble of protest from among the workmen. "You can't—you *wouldn't*—dare to do such a barbaric thing."

"I not only *can,* I *would*—and *will,"* the Englishman declared and his eyes roamed over the nervous, perturbed group of civilians. Returning his gaze to Fletcher, he pointed. "Take that one. And the big, fat bastard. His neck ought pop as sweet as can be when we whip the horse from under him."

Without speaking, Red and Kiowa moved forward. The civilians began to protest, but the rest of the soldiers kept their weapons held in a threatening manner that overrode any hope of more strenuous objections. Closing on the designated pair, the two Texans shoved them none too gently from their companions.

"You can't do this to us!" Fletcher wailed, then glared at Dusty. "Stop them, damn you!"

"Show me how I can!" the small Texan answered, sounding desperate.

"Tell them what they want to know!" Fletcher replied. "That's how."

"I—I can't!" Dusty groaned.

"Come on. Let's have some movement there," Staunce commanded. "Get them to the trees and haul them up."

Joined by two more soldiers, Red and Kiowa made as if to hustle the selected civilians away. Fletcher moved, but Meats stood still.

"Let me talk to you," the burly man requested, looking from Staunce to the suspended, still kicking, figures hanging from the tree.

"What about?" the Englishman asked.

"In private," Meats requested, sweat pouring down his face as it took on a pleading expression. "Please, captain, it's important. You'll regret it if you don't hear me out."

"All right," Staunce said, sounding reluctant. "What is it?"

"Not here," Meats began.

"Go and hang him!" Staunce barked.

"Damn it!" Meats howled, wild with anger and alarm, as the two soldiers once more pretended to be eager to carry out their orders. "I'm a member of the Union's Secret Service—"

"Oh sure," Staunce sniffed. "And I'm President Lincoln."

"It's true I tell you!" Meats insisted. "Last night I crossed the Ouachita and brought back some posters that I've got to spread around Camden. Let me take you to where I've hidden them."

"Well now," Staunce answered, resuming his normal way of speaking. "I hardly think you need to do that. Do you, Dusty?"

Shock twisted at Meats' features and his cheeks reddened in rage as he realized that he had been tricked into making a damning confession. His eyes swung from the

"Yankee" captain to the Confederate "first lieutenant" and back.

"Why you—!" Meats began, tensing.

"Stay put, *hombre!*" Kiowa Cotton advised and his face was sufficiently menacing to ensure compliance with the request.

Again excited chatter arose among the civilians. They were becoming aware that things were vastly different to what had appeared on the surface. The "shot" soldiers were rising, grinning amiably at their "killers." At the edge of the woodland, more of the "Yankees" were raising the suspended pair and removing the ropes from their necks.

Dusty was watching the latter operation with considerable interest and not a little anxiety. It was with much relief that he saw Hassle and the other man had not been injured. While the leather harnesses they had worn—each provided with metal hooks under which the noose had been placed and prevented from closing about the throat—were strong and had been tested by Dusty himself before being used, things might still have gone wrong. Certainly the pair deserved every commendation for volunteering to take that particular part in the scheme.

"That was a neat trick, young feller," Fletcher praised and nodded to where Kiowa was guarding Meats. "He's a feller I was wanting to meet. I thought all along he might be, he was too loyal to the South to be true."

"How do you mean?" Staunce inquired, the words having been directed at him.

"I'm with the Confederate Secret Service," Fletcher explained. "We heard that there're Yankee spies along the Ouachita and I was sent to try to get to know them. That was why I acted like I've been doing. I figured the spy might reckon I'd be useful to him. Lord, though, you had me worried. Everything that happened looked so damned real."

"Yes, it did," Dusty said thoughtfully and gingerly touched his reddened cheek. He looked to where his cousin had handed the Springfield carbine—which had sent the bullet between his feet—to a genuine private and was watching Hassle's party. "Red."

"Ye—" the redhead began, turning.

Gliding forward, Dusty whipped up his right hand. The knuckles took Red under the jaw and, although Dusty had not struck with his full strength, dumped the surprised youngster rump-first on the ground.

"Hey!" Red yelped indignantly. "What was that for?"

"Hitting me the way you did," Dusty answered, extending his open right hand.

"But you said for me to hit you!" Red protested as his cousin helped him back to his feet.

"Sure," Dusty agreed. "But I didn't say you should *enjoy* doing it."

## CHAPTER SEVEN

## We Could Lose Everything

From the moment Dusty Fog entered the library of the fine colonial-style house, loaned by a prominent Camden citizen for use as General Hardin's temporary headquarters, he sensed that events had taken a very serious turn. It showed on the faces of his father, Ole Devil, Colonel Blaze and Major Smith. Almost instinctively, Dusty guessed what was wrong. The older men were gathered about the big desk and, prominent on it, were the warning notices which he and Captain Staunce had found beyond Stilton Crossing.

The time was shortly after ten o'clock at night. Having left Lieutenant Clements and his men to resume their interrupted guard duties—they had been hidden in the woods while the deception was being played out—Dusty had brought Meats to the jail in Camden. During the journey, the spy had been questioned. None of his answers had been very informative. However, Dusty had felt that any threat Meats might have posed was now at an end.

Unless, of course—

"The Mounted Infantry haven't dealt with the big gun, Dustine," Ole Devil announced, raising the matter upon which his nephew had just been dwelling. "They'd crossed the river about two miles upstream from Arkadelphia and were taking a roundabout route to join the Malvern trail behind the woods. Instead, they were ambushed by a large force of Yankee cavalry using repeating rifles and suffered heavy losses."

That meant, Dusty realized, only the warning notices had been prevented from making their appearances. The bombardment could still be carried out. The situation was very grave and he had been correct in his guess at what was causing the solemn expressions displayed by his superiors. They had returned from Arkadelphia knowing that a serious and dangerous threat must be met.

"Only one officer escaped," Colonel Blaze went on. "A young shavetail.* He'd been wounded and wasn't too coherent. But, from what he said, it looks as if the Yankees knew they were coming and had been waiting for them."

"How about the gun, sir?" Dusty asked.

"They never saw it," Ole Devil answered. "But the commanding officer of the detachment across the Ouachita sent a message under a flag of truce. He apologized on behalf of the Union Army for the shelling and assured us that it wouldn't happen again."

"Do you believe him, sir?" Dusty inquired.

"He's a career soldier and a man of honour," Blaze put in. "I know him. He wouldn't have allowed the shelling to happen if he'd known about it."

"But, according to these notices, it was done as part of a plan to make us turn General Culver loose," Dusty objected. "Surely he'd have been told about it, sir."

"One would think so," Blaze conceded. "But I'm inclined to believe he wasn't. The order could have come from higher up and, knowing that many of their officers wouldn't approve, they didn't spread the word around."

"That's possible," Ole Devil went on. "Has that damned spy been questioned yet?"

"We asked him a few, sir," Dusty admitted.

"I won't inquire *how* you asked," the general promised, frosty black eyes raking his small nephew from head to toe.

"*Gracias,* sir," Dusty replied, thinking of the methods he had applied. The torture had been far more anticipatory than actual, with the victim being led to expect far worse lay ahead if he failed to co-operate. "He wasn't more than a messenger, though, and had only claimed to be a member of the Yankees' Secret Service to impress our 'blue-bellies' with his importance. Mr. Fletcher's inclined to think he

---

*Shavetail: derogatory name for a second lieutenant.

was telling the truth. Anyways, Meats reckons that he'd been told to watch for a signal from the other side, then row over. When he got there, he was given the bundle. He was to put out some of the posters around Camden tomorrow evening, then start to move down the river and leave more of them at the villages along the way."

"And *you* believe him?" asked Ole Devil.

"I reckon he was too scared of Kiowa and Vern Hassle to lie," Dusty replied. "And what he said made sense. He told us he'd left the bundle under the boat instead of taking it along straight away because he didn't have to start putting out the notices until tomorrow evening and figured it would be safer there than around his bunk at the camp. If anybody should've found the boat, there was nothing to show he'd been near it."

"That sounds reasonable and likely," Hondo Fog stated.

"So the big gun won't be here until tomorrow evening," Ole Devil said, tapping a finger on the poster.

"Or the day after, sir," Dusty suggested. "They'd have to haul it up from Arkadelphia and that won't be done at speed. And they'll want folks to have seen the posters before they start throwing the shells, so that you can be asked to set General Culver free."

"Assuming, of course, that their main purpose is to set Culver free," Ole replied. "It could be that they are hoping to use the threat of the big gun to make us go back across the Ouachita and face them in open battle."

"That, even more than securing Culver's release, may be what the Union's high command wants," Blaze went on. "A decisive action in which we could lose everything, or be so weakened that they can discount us as a factor in the War."

"Are the Yankees ready to fight a major action, sir?" Dusty wanted to know. "After all, we're holding their commanding general and they can't have replaced him yet."

"From the reports I've had, Culver was more figurehead than commanding general," Ole Devil replied. "And, even without him, there may be colonels with sufficient knowledge and ambition to make this play."

"Which means that we must find some way of destroying the big gun," Blaze declared. "And *before* we're compelled to take mass action, if possible. But, considering what happened to the Mounted Infantry, it won't be easy."

"I reckon they were seen almost as soon as they crossed the river by the observer in the balloon," Dusty guessed, when the colonel paused and every eye turned on him as if seeking his opinion. "That meant they had time to move their cavalry screen into position to ambush the Mounted Infantry."

"It's probably what happened," Blaze conceded. "So we'll have to send a large enough force, two or three Companies, next time."

"With respect, sir," Dusty said quietly, stiffening into a brace and holding his voice to a flat, yet respectful tone. "I don't think a larger force is the answer."

"Why not?" Blaze asked.

"The bigger the force, even if they split up, the greater chance of it being located by the men in the balloon," Dusty explained. "Seeing that we know now which way they're headed, a single Company might be able to handle it."

"*Your* Company, I suppose, Dustine," Ole Devil put in.

"Not necessarily, sir," Dusty replied. "But Company 'C' is at full strength and—well, I'd been figuring on taking them on a long training ride, so they're armed, supplied and ready to go. I reckon we could handle it."

None of the older men spoke for several seconds, but all studied the small, blond youngster. Dusty had already reverted to his more comfortable, non-issue style of dress and, without any suggestion of being cocky or self-assured, he exuded a quiet aura of confidence. If he was sent on the mission and failed, it would not be through rashness or a lack of thought and planning ability.

Behind a cold mask that hid all emotion, Ole Devil was deeply concerned. He knew that the threat of the big gun must be removed as quickly as possible. If it was not, it could easily turn the scales in the Union's favour. To send Dusty across the Ouachita might cause his death; but the same applied no matter which officer received the assignment and the general knew them all as well as he did his small, blond nephew.

The question facing Ole Devil was whether Dusty could carry out the mission. The general was inclined to believe that he could. Regard for his favourite nephew's safety could not be allowed to affect the decision. Ever since Dusty had joined the regiment, he had proven himself a capable, courageous and intelligent officer and leader. All three qualities had been amply displayed in how he had dealt with the affair at Stilton Crossing. While Dusty had had Captain Staunce's assistance, the main plan had been his own. What was more, the youngster had insisted upon personally testing both sets of harness before allowing them to be used in creating a convincing and effective part of the deception.

"Very well, Dustine," the general said, trying to keep his voice hard and impersonal. "You will take your Company and destroy the big gun."

"Yo!" Dusty assented, unable to suppress the eagerness he was feeling.

Although Hondo Fog shared the general's concern for his son's future, he forced himself to carry out his duty.

"When do you plan to move out, Dusty?" Hondo inquired.

"Before midnight, if I can, sir," the small Texan replied. "Or as soon as I can after. I want to be well beyond the river by sun-up, so that I can come at them from behind. They'll be less likely to expect us from that direction."

"That's good thinking, Dustine," Colonel Blaze praised. "Is there anything you need by way of supplies?"

"No, sir," Dusty replied. "Like I said, I've had the men set for a three-day ride. We've everything we need. Except maybe—"

"Well?" Blaze prompted.

"Could I ask Captain Staunce to come with me, sir?"

"You mean you want to take his mountain battery?" asked Ole Devil.

"Yes, sir. Those little wheel-guns of his throw a shell for over half a mile and, with his men handling them, come real close to hitting what they're aimed at. They could make our work a whole heap easier and more certain."

"Won't they slow you down, or be awkward to take across the river?" Hondo wanted to know.

"I don't think so," Dusty answered. "We'll not be travelling too far at a gallop and, if we have to, we can get them across on boats. I've another reason for wanting Doug—Captain Staunce along. The big gun won't be too far from the river. We might just be able to capture it and fetch it back with us."

"There's not a whole lot of hope of *that*," Blaze warned.

"No, sir." Dusty conceded. "But, happen the chance comes, I'd like to be ready for it. And Captain Staunce knows a heap more than I do about moving a cannon."

"Very well," Ole Devil confirmed. "Take him and his battery with you. But don't forget that your primary objective is to *destroy* the big gun, not to try to capture it."

Affirming that he understood his duty, Dusty discussed a few other points and then left the building. Mounting his horse, he rode to the Texas Light Cavalry's camp. As he approached the wall-tent which he was sharing with his second-in-command, Red came out. Red was dressed, apart from his hat, tunic and weapon belt.

"Is everything ready for tomorrow, Cousin Red?" Dusty asked, remaining on the bay's back.

"Why sure," agreed the redhead, without displaying any great enthusiasm. "Fifty rounds a man for the revolvers, same for their shoulder arms. Food for three days, just like you told me."

*"Bueno,"* Dusty said.

"Do we *have* to take that damned ride?" Red asked, for he was not looking forward with any pleasure to carrying out the long training march which Dusty had arranged.

"Nope," the small Texan replied, watching his cousin with amused anticipation and awaiting his reaction to the word.

"Maybe we ought to get them doing some shoot—" Red began, then realized what Dusty's answer had been. "Did you say *'no'?"*

"That's just what I said. Get your horse and go ask Doug Staunce if he and his Limeys would like to come along with us and see how a good horse-outfit does its work. Tell him Uncle Devil reckons the exercise will do them good."

"Yo! What's doing—Just happen Doug wants to know?"

"We're going over the Ouachita after the big gun," Dusty explained and was delighted by the expression that crossed his cousin's face. "Tell Doug that I'm hoping to be moving out by one o'clock, if not sooner."

Leaving Red, who dived back into the tent to dress before setting off with the message, Dusty made his way to his enlisted men's quarters. Going to the tent assigned to the senior non-commissioned officers, he found only the sergeant major present.

"Turn out the Company, Billy Jack," Dusty ordered as the lanky figure came in answer to his call. "Have the bugler sound 'Boots and Saddles.'"

"Yo!" Billy Jack replied. "Only most of the new men've gone down to the Tavern. They were paid and I figured they wouldn't be wanted before morning."

"That's all right," Dusty said. "You weren't to know."

"I'll go fetch them—"

"Leave that to me, you have the others making ready."

"Livesey's not going to be too happy about you taking them away while they've still got money in their pockets," Billy Jack warned. "I'd step careful, was I you, Cap'n Dusty. His uncle's the mayor."

"I'll bear it in mind and be *real* polite," Dusty promised. "Have that big black gelding we took from the Lancers for me to use, this bay's been pushed hard recently."

"Yo!" the sergeant major assented, but did not make an immediate start to commencing his duties. "I could fetch Kiowa and Stormy Weather from the pok—prayer meeting they're at and have them come with you."

"Tell them to come down after me," Dusty suggested.

For all his mournful appearance and habit of always pretending to expect doom and disaster, Dusty knew that

Billy Jack was no alarmist. If he felt that the owner of the Tavern might prove to be difficult, the small Texan was willing to accept his summation.

Having accepted Billy Jack's offer, Dusty set his mount into motion. Holding the bay to a canter, he wasted no time in covering the half mile separating the camp from Camden. Once there, he made his way towards the river. The Tavern stood about fifty yards from the bank, a one floor stone building glowing with light and the sounds of merriment. Looking across the water, Dusty could see little or no signs of life. As at Arkadelphia, the Yankees had halted at long cannon shot and there was only the red glare of their camp fires to tell of their presence.

At that moment, Dusty was not especially interested in the enemy. Instead, he swung his gaze to the horses hitched to the rail outside the Tavern. They all bore double-girthed Texas saddles, which meant they would be available for use by his men.

Swinging from the bay, Dusty left it ground-hitched. He crossed the warped board-walk, opened the front door and entered the barroom. Smoke hung in a heavy cloud under the roof, being combatted by the lamps which illuminated the tables and bar. A number of garishly-attired girls hung around the soldiers who appeared to be the majority of the customers, encouraging them to drink, or take part in the various gambling games. There were half a dozen burly, hard-looking civilians, who had the appearance of river roughnecks, scattered around and watching the various activities with more than casual interest. Behind the bar, two big, tough-faced men attended to the customers' needs.

Looking around, Dusty discovered that the majority of the soldiers were recruits. Half of them belonged to his Company, replacements for the men who had died at Martin's Mill. However, standing at the bar and gazing about him in a tolerant manner, Corporal Vern Hassle held a glass of whiskey.

Dusty's arrival created some interest among the civilians in the room. It also was arousing suspicion, he guessed. The Tavern was not often visited by officers, being an establishment devoted to the enlisted men. So the bartenders, girls and roughnecks were wondering what had brought him into their presence.

"Hello, handsome," greeted a pretty girl, leaving two lanky recruits who were part of Company 'C' and approaching the small Texan. "My name's Magda. Is there anything I can do for you?"

"Not off hand, ma'am," Dusty replied, partially gratified for the silence that had fallen over the room. "You men from Company 'C,' finish your drinks and get mounted. We're going back to camp."

A chorus of protest rolled up. Although the recruits recognized Dusty and had heard plenty about him from the old hands, they had seen little of him since joining his Company. So they were not over impressed—having taken sufficient drinks for their susceptibilities to have become dulled—as he stood there, a small figure amongst so many bigger, older men.

"Hey!" said one of the pair who had been entertaining Magda, standing and picking up a bottle. Crossing the room behind Dusty, he draped his other arm around the captain's shoulders in a friendly manner. "You take a drin—"

Which was as far as the recruit got.

Dusty knew that, with the soldiers in their present frame of mind, he could not permit the man to take such liberties. If he did, he would have no control over any of them. So he acted with his usual speed and effectiveness.

Raising his right boot, Dusty propelled its heel hard against the top of the soldier's left foot. With a shrill yelp of pain, the recipient of the attack jerked away his arm and hopped on his other leg. Turning, Dusty laid the palm of his right hand against the man's face and shoved. Reeling backwards, the soldier sat down hard on the floor with the bottle flying out of his hand.

"Like I said," Dusty announced, giving no indication of knowing that the recruit had come and gone. "I want every man from Company 'C'—"

One of the biggest civilians lurched forward. Hooking his thumbs in his waist belt, he loomed above the small Texan and teetered menacingly on his heels.

"Now just a blasted minute," the man snarled. "This ain't no son-of-a-bitching Army camp. You ain't got no right—"

"This's an Army matter, mister," Dusty interrupted. "So—"

"Like hell it is!" the man barked back. "Them things on your sleeves don't pack no weight in here."

"I'd best apologize now," Dusty said quietly.

"So you should, coming in here—"

"No," Dusty corrected. "For what I'm going to do to you."

And saying it, he kicked the man sharply but with considerable force on the front of the shin bone. Letting out a startled and agonized howl, the roughneck went backwards, hopping on his uninjured limb. He did not go far enough. Advancing almost with a bound, Dusty whipped over a right cross that slammed his knuckles into the side of the man's jaw. How hard the punch landed was shown by the bulky figure changing course with rapidity. Blundering away from his assailant, he landed belly down on top of a table which collapsed under his weight. Almost before the man's body had reached the floor, Dusty's matched Colts were drawn to throw down on others of the civilians. However, he could not watch everybody in the room.

Behind the counter, one of the bartenders reached to where he kept a shot-gun with its barrels cut down to a convenient length. Before his fingers closed about the butt, he heard a double click and a cracked, old voice addressing him.

"There ain't nothing down there's you wants, now be there, friend?"

Raising his gaze, the bartender looked into the yawning muzzle of a Dragoon Colt and beyond it was the leathery, ancient face of Corporal Hassle. Old the non-com might be, but the heavy revolver never wavered in its alignment.

"Nope," conceded the bartender, bringing his hands hurriedly into view. "There ain't."

The front door opened to admit Kiowa Cotton and the

stocky, powerful Sergeant "Stormy" Weather. They each held a revolver and changed the minds of two other civilians who had considered drawing weapons.

"Like I said," Dusty barked, returning the Colts to their holsters almost as swiftly as he had drawn them. "I want every man of my Com—"

"One minute!" called a voice and a tall, elegantly-dressed man came from a doorway at the rear of the room. "These soldiers are here as my guests and I question your right to come in giving them orders."

"They're in the Army—," Dusty began, guessing correctly that he was speaking to Livesey, the owner.

"And they're on civilian property," Livesey countered, taking in the bare details of Dusty's appearance without looking at the essentials. Believing that he was dealing with a callow, inexperienced junior officer, he decided to try a bluff and continued bombastically, "I resent this high-handed attitude and won't hesitate to lodge a complaint with Colonel Blaze, or even General Hardin. My uncle is mayor of Camden—"

"And I'm General Hardin's and Colonel Blaze's nephew," Dusty put in, watching alarm come to the man's face. "My name is Fog."

For a moment Livesey stared at the small Texan and this time took notice of the triple gold bars on his collar. The Tavern's owner had heard of Dusty and knew that he was related to the senior officers in question. So, while Livesey hated to see the recruits leave before they had spent all their money, he decided that it would not be polite, or wise, to antagonize a man with such influential family connections.

"The bar's closed to all members of Captain Fog's Company," Livesey declared, putting on a more benevolent expression than he was feeling. "There'll be a free drink for every one of you next time you come in, but now I want to see you all obeying orders and getting going."

"Why thank you 'most to death, sir," Dusty drawled, watching the soldiers rise and start to file out. "It's sure good to see such a co-operative gentleman."

With that, the small Texan strolled from the room. He neither saw nor would have cared if he had seen, the bitter glare the owner threw after him. Instead, he was thinking of the work that lay ahead. Luckily none of his men were too drunk to ride. Something told him that he might need every one of them before he was finished with the big gun.

## CHAPTER EIGHT

# That "Young Feller"'s a Gal

Although a well-bred young Southron lady was expected to ride side-saddle, Harriet Cable had gained considerable proficiency in sitting astride a horse. Her earlier defiance of convention had proved to be of the greatest assistance in the days that had followed her escape from her home on Nimrod Lake.

Having taken the boat almost to Perryville, Harry and her Negro companion had left it before reaching the town. They had made their way on foot to the Bluchers' home. There it had been the girl's unpleasant duty to inform Mrs. Blucher of her husband's death. Harry had not seen the duel, but had heard about it from the butler. At his wife's instigation, Oscar had hidden in the garden and watched what happened through the window. Despite her horror, shock and grief, Mrs. Blucher was of sturdy pioneering stock. So she had held her emotions in check while helping the girl to make preparations for the journey.

Supplied with horses from Bluchers' stables, Harry and Eric had set off to try to find her father. They had headed south, following the headwaters of the Saline River to Benson. From there, acting upon the information they had gathered, they had crossed the river and ridden parallel to—but out of sight of—the trail to Malvern. All the time they had been riding, they had kept a careful watch for any pursuers Major Lyle might have dispatched to capture them. While there had been a few Union patrols, Harry and Eric had avoided being seen by them. Nor had they appeared to be searching for the girl and her Negro escort.

One thing had soon become obvious. The Yankees had attempted to keep Pulling Sue's purpose a secret. They had only been partially successful. Faced with the restrictions placed upon their movements by the Union Army, none of the friends Harry had contacted in the various towns could help her to locate her father. So that task had fallen upon Eric's broad, capable shoulders and he had been more successful. Not only was he large, brawny and intelligent, he was also Mama Lukie's son. The Cable family's cook had a reputation throughout Arkansas as being a conjure-woman of considerable potency. On learning Eric's identity, the Negroes he had questioned were ready to render every possible assistance. So, with their help, Harry had been able to trace her father's movements. She had also been able to discover how the war was progressing and keep in touch with its latest developments.

Acting upon the information gathered by her companion, Harry had made her way towards Arkadelphia. However, instead of trying to cross the Ouachita River, they had turned downstream and made for Camden.

Shortly after noon one day, the girl and the Negro found themselves riding along the bottom of a broad, winding valley. They had selected the route to avoid being seen on a sky-line. While they were still a good two miles north of the river, they had felt that it was not advisable to go any nearer.

The bank was certain to be patrolled by the Yankees. By that time, word of their escape could have been circulated and the girl had not wanted to attract unwanted interest or attentions. If her father was anywhere in the vicinity, she would know about it without needing to see him; Pulling Sue would ensure that.

Suddenly two figures appeared, ahead and on the right hand side of the valley. Although mounted, they had concealed themselves amongst the bushes that coated the slopes so successfully that they had remained undetected by Harry or Eric until showing themselves in a silent, but alarming manner.

With a sickening sense of failure, Harry saw that the men wore U.S. Cavalry uniforms. Her first instinct was to send her horse galloping along the valley in the hope of dashing by. Next she considered attempting to turn and make a run for safety in the other direction. Clearly Eric was duplicating her feelings.

"What're we going to do, Miss Harry?" the Negro inquired, sounding nervous. He knew that many Union Army soldiers would be suspicious, even indignant, at finding a white girl riding in the company of a coloured man. While supposedly fighting to liberate the slaves, they objected to too close contact between the objects of their efforts and their own women. "Go like bats out of hell?"

Instead of replying immediately, Harry gave a few seconds of rapid but careful thought to the situation. Her father had always stressed the need to do so in times of danger and she respected his superior wisdom. Swiftly she studied the approaching riders and formed her conclusions.

One was sufficiently sinister looking to be worthy of alarm and concern; being Indian-dark and savage-featured, despite the sergeant's chevrons on his sleeves. Older, shorter and white-haired, the other seemed less frightening and sported the insignia of a corporal. While their clothing was typical of the United States' Cavalry, which was well on the way to standardizing its uniforms, they wore gun-belts with revolvers in open-topped holsters and their saddles were not of the McClellan pattern. Each carried a Henry repeating rifle across the crook of his left arm. While they made no attempt to move the weapons to a position of greater readiness, doing so would not be a lengthy process.

Having taken the last point into consideration, Harry realized that flight would avail them little or nothing. The horses she and Eric were riding had been pushed hard since leaving Perryville. Those of the two soldiers looked fresh and in the peak of physical condition. From the easy, relaxed way the men sat their saddles, they were probably far better riders, too. Even if they were not, she suspected that they were sufficiently skilled with their rifles to render any attempts at escape dangerous, if not fatal.

The pair's appearances—apart from the sergeant's menacing face—were another point Harry noticed. They looked fairly neat and tidy, which suggested that they were not deserters. If they had been, the girl would have been very worried. Deserters had built up an ugly reputation during the War years. Maybe the sergeant looked as mean as all hell, but there was an amiable, perky, almost disarmingly friendly air about the white-haired corporal.

Lastly, the girl noticed that the soldiers seemed surprised and puzzled by seeing her. Certainly they gave no hint of having been searching for her and Eric.

"Wait!" Harry decided. "They may not be looking for us and we might learn where Poppa is."

With that, the girl brought her horse to a stop. Eric reined in slightly behind her. There was, he conceded, no hope of dashing by the soldiers or turning around to run away. Already the men had reached the valley bottom and were approaching, spreading apart, along it.

"Howdy, you-all," greeted the corporal, halting his wolf-grey *bayo-lobo* gelding about ten yards ahead of the couple. "Real pleasant afternoon."

At the corporal's side, the dark-featured sergeant said nothing. Instead he studied Harry with cold, wary eyes.

For her part, Harry stiffened slightly. The old timer's accent was that of a Texan. While the Lone Star State was part of the Confederacy some of its people had elected to fight for the North. So the discovery did not raise any hope in her breast.

"Howdy fellers," the girl replied disturbed by the sergeant's continued scrutiny but forcing herself to adopt a husky and—she hoped—masculine timbre in her voice. "It sure is."

In addition to trying to sound like a boy, Harry hoped that the combination of the broad-brimmed hat—under which she had tucked all her hair—wolfskin jacket, boy's shirt, trousers and riding boots would prevent her real sex from being discovered. However, in case the soldiers meant mischief, she slipped her right hand casually into the jacket's pocket and closed it around the butt of the Colt Pocket Pistol.

"Mind if I asks where you're going, young feller?" the corporal went on and the girl's relief at apparently having succeeded in her attempt at deception was lessened by the sergeant's continued, silent examination. Not that his face offered her any clue to his feelings. There was an almost apologetic note in the old timer's voice as he continued, "It ain't none of my never-mind, I'll grant you, but when you gets to my age, you're entitled to act all nosey."

"Eric and me," Harry replied, continuing to use her "male" voice, "we're looking to enlist and fight the Rebs. Reckon your outfit'd take us on?"

"I dunno about that, young *feller*," answered the corporal, laying a little emphasis on the last word. "But I'd admire to see you take your hand out of the pocket. When you gets to my age, you're kind of nervous about folks's finger guns when they're talking to you."

"When you gets to your age, I'd say your eyes start to go back on you, Vern," the sergeant put in and, although harsh and somewhat guttural, he too spoke with a pronounced Texas drawl. "That 'young feller' 's a gal."

"I knowed *that* all along, ye danged whipper-snapper!" the corporal yelped, bristling with indignation yet maintaining his vigilance. "Only I thought's how the young lady was trying to make us think otherwise, us being Texas gentlemen—leastways, *one* of us be—we should reckon we'd been fooled."

"Likely," grunted the sergeant and his cold eyes seemed to be boring into Harry's head. "'Cepting he talks a heap too much, ma'am, Vern had him a right smart point. I'd admire to see an *empty* hand come out of that pocket right now."

"All right," the girl sighed, yielding to the inevitable and complying with what had clearly been a demand rather than a request. Realizing the deception had failed, she reverted to her normal manner of speaking.

"That's a heap more neighbourly," commented the corporal. "So you're looking to enlist in the Yankee Army, huh?"

"You two did," Harry countered, although she was starting to have doubts on that point.

"Well now, I'll tell you, ma'am," the old timer answered, contriving to look and sound as if he was thoroughly ashamed of what he was about to confess. "We ain't *exactly* in the *Yankee* Army. Fact being, there's some's might say we was out-'n'-out 'impostlers.'"

"Who are you?" Harry asked, guessing the man had meant "impostors." "And what are you doing out here?"

"Names're Vern Hassle, which's me," the corporal introduced, "'n' Kiowa Cotton. Ranks're right, but we belongs to Company 'C,' of the Texas Light Cavalry, ma'am. Like I said, there's some might call us 'impostlers.' And, from the way you're dressed and've been talking, I'd be just a leetle mite inclined to say we're not the only ones."

"That's true," Harry conceded, but she did not know whether to be pleased or distressed by meeting two members of the Confederate States' Army.

## CHAPTER NINE

# We're Headed in the Wrong Direction

Although nothing showed on Sergeant Kiowa Cotton's face, he was very interested. From the first moment he and Corporal Hassle had discovered that Harry was a girl, before they had shown themselves, they had been puzzled by her presence. Wanting to learn more about her—and being confident that there were no Yankee soldiers in the vicinity —they had decided to announce their true identity and see what response that brought. Kiowa had guessed that they had made the right decision when he heard her speaking with the accent of a well-bred Southron.

"I'm not nosey, like some, ma'am," Kiowa remarked, favouring his ancient companion with a cold glare. "But Cap'n Fog, him being our Company's commanding officer, he's going to want to know who you are and why you're fixing to enlist in the Yankee Army."

"We're riding scout for Company 'C,' ma'am," Hassle continued. "And, like Kiowa said, Cap'n Fog's going to want to talk to you. So, happen you've no objections, you'd best come along and meet him."

"I've no objections," Harry smiled, sensing that she could trust the two soldiers and would be safe in their company. There was, however, something that she felt must be settled. "Eric's a free man. Poppa set his folks free long before the War."

"We'll mind it, ma'am," Kiowa promised, knowing that such had frequently been done even by people who were now supporting the Confederate cause. "Happen you reckon you can find the way. Vern, being so damned old an all, you'd best take them. I'll keep looking for that blasted old gun."

"Big gun!" Harry repeated, throwing a glance at Eric, then trying to compose her features into an expression of merely casual inquiry. "Is that what you're looking for?"

"Yes'm," Hassle confirmed, watching her with what might have been no more than ordinary interest. "That's just what we're after. You wouldn't've seen the son-of-a-bit— consarned and blasted thing, now would you?"

"No," Harry was forced to admit, in what she hoped would be tones of mere curiosity.

She felt that it was advisable to refrain from mentioning her connection with the big gun until after she had met the soldiers' commanding officer. After all, she had only their unsupported words regarding their true status.

"I didn't reckon we'd be *that* lucky," Hassle sighed, glancing at his companion. "Don't you go letting them blasted Yankees catch you, Kiowa."

"I'll do what I can to stop 'em," the sergeant promised and, nodding to the girl, set his big roan gelding into motion. "See you later, Vern. Unless you up and die of old age afore I get back."

"When you get's old's me, it could happen," the corporal pointed out to Kiowa's departing back. Then he turned his attention to the girl. "We'll sort of keep to the low ground and sneak about kind of careful, if that be all right with you, ma'am. I know I'm dressed like a Yankee, but seeing you two along could make any of 'em's happened to see us mighty suspicious."

"We're in your hands," Harry confirmed, having taken a liking to the old timer and concluded that he was anything but as decrepit as he liked to suggest.

Taking the precautions suggested by Hassle, the girl and the Negro accompanied him. They traversed almost two miles without seeing anything to alarm them. Little was said as they rode along. The girl was wondering what the corporal had made of finding her travelling alone except for Eric, but his leathery old face had not given her a hint as to his thoughts. There was another item which insisted on passing through her head. She had only Hassle's word that he did not belong to the United States' Army. Perhaps he had been lying and was merely escorting her into captivity.

If Harry had known it, Hassle was more concerned at that time with keeping a watch for Yankee patrols. Who she was and what she might be doing could, in his considered opinion, be settled more satisfactorily and safely after they had rejoined Company "C."

"Won't be long now, ma'am," Hassle commented at last, having given the surrounding terrain an even more thorough and careful scrutiny, as they approached a stretch of woodland. "The Company's hid away in there. You see, we're not exactly in Confederate territory and Yankees ain't noted for Southron hospitality. So Cap'n Fog allowed we shouldn't let 'em know we're around."

"This Captain Fog sounds a right smart man," Harry remarked with a smile, for she had noticed the sound of respect which had accompanied every mention of the officer's name made by the two soldiers. Her situation would be greatly helped if she had fallen in with a capable officer, one who could understand the full significance of her position.

"He's all of that, ma'am," the corporal confirmed.

On reaching the first of the trees, Harry saw an alert, watchful sentry behind the trunk of an oak. He wore the uniform of the Confederate States' Cavalry and his kepi carried the badge which she identified as being of the Texas Light Cavalry. Giving a cheery wave as they rode by, he turned his attention once more to gazing at the land before him.

Going deeper into the woodland, the girl came upon hobbled horses, watched over by more members of the Texas Light Cavalry. However, the main body of Company "C" appeared to be sleeping. They lay, rolled in their blankets and using their saddles for pillows, in whatever cover or shelter they had found.

"Some folks've all the danged luck," Hassle complained and, disregarding the fact that he had volunteered for the assignment, went on, "Sending a poor, wored-out old cuss like me to do the dirty work while they lies sleeping."

"It's a sin and shame!" Harry declared indignantly, her compassion aroused by what appeared to be a genuine, heart-felt protestation.

"Anyways, none of us got any sleep last night and young 'n's need it more 'n' old timers like me," Hassle grinned and heard the girl give an annoyed snort as she realized she had been tricked. "There's Cap'n Fog."

Turning in the direction indicated by her escort, Harry saw a small, blond officer throwing aside his blankets and rising. For a moment, she wondered if the corporal had made a mistake, or if she was looking the wrong way. She had expected Captain Fog to be a much older, more impressive man. Yet there did not appear to be another officer present. However, not far away, a tall, gangling, mournful-faced sergeant major had also woken and was rising.

"Don't tell me you've found the big gun already, Vern?" Captain Dusty Fog inquired, throwing a quick look at the girl and the Negro but dealing with what he regarded as the more important matter first.

"Can't come out truthful and say we have, Cap'n Dusty," Hassle confessed. "Met up with this young lady, though, 'n' concluded you'd like to see 'em."

"Howdy, ma'am," Dusty greeted Harry. "Get down, please."

Before the girl could follow the small Texan's instructions, she heard the sound of fast-running hooves. A rider was galloping recklessly through the trees from the opposite direction to which the girl's party had arrived. He was a tall, well-built red-haired young first lieutenant, Harry observed and looked excited or considerably agitated.

"We're headed in the wrong direction, Cousin Dusty!" Red Blaze announced, bringing his big brown gelding to a sliding halt and quitting its saddle almost in the same motion. "That damned balloon's just going up back across the river from Camden."

"The hell it is!" Dusty ejaculated, exchanging a startled glance with Sergeant Major Billy Jack. "How can it be? No team of horses could have hauled it from Arkadelphia that quickly."

"They'd've left a string of dead 'n's behind for the turkey buzzards, even had they worked them in relays," Billy Jack went on, but without any of his usual gloomy predictions. He only employed them when things were going right.

The news brought by Red suggested that things had gone badly wrong.

In some way, Dusty appeared to have fallen into the trap of having underestimated the enemy. Working on the assumption that the big gun's weight and general unwieldiness would have caused it to be travelling very slowly, he had brought his men over Ouachita River about three miles upstream from Stilton Crossing. They had left the vicinity of the bank immediately and, by the time dawn had broken, they had covered four more miles in a north-westerly direction. Daylight had found them concealed in the woodland and resting. Dusty had taken the precaution in case the Yankees should have had their balloon in the air. For miles around, the nature of the terrain was too open for him to chance moving such a large body of men, horses and the four little mountain howitzers across it. Instead, he had dispatched his two best scouts, dressed as Yankees—there had not been sufficient uniforms to supply all his Company and Staunce's battery—to try to locate the big gun. Having seen that his men were all right, the Englishman had joined Red with the small rear guard. They had been watching in case the Yankees had discovered that enemies were north of the Ouachita and had come looking for them.

Despite all the precautions and the hard work entailed in transporting the howitzers over the river, using four rowing boats held by the guard at Stilton Crossing, it seemed that Dusty had miscalculated. The men with the big gun had contrived to pass through the territory which his scouts were searching and, in a remarkably short time, had already reached their destination.

"After the raid you pulled on their remount depot at Searcy, I'd've sworn that the Yankees didn't have enough spare horses to kill them off reckless-like," Red told his cousin sympathetically, watching Harry, Hassle and Eric dismounting. Although consumed with curiosity regarding the girl, he kept his mind on the serious development at hand. "And, like Billy Jack said, they'd've had to kill off plenty to get the gun up Camden way so quickly."

Sucking in a deep breath, the girl prepared to face the moment she had been dreading ever since learning Hassle's real identity and hearing of Company "C's" mission.

"They aren't using horses to pull it," Harry said.

"They have to be!" Red protested. "There's no railroad hereabouts and we'd have heard if they were using a steamboat along the river. And they sure's hell aren't hauling it with men on the ropes."

"How are they moving it, ma'am?" Dusty asked and, quietly as he spoke, the girl suddenly became aware of the full strength of his personality.

In some strange fashion, the small Texan seemed to Harry to have taken on stature until he towered above his companions. She knew that it was only an illusion, but she would never again think of Dusty Fog as being small.

"With a traction engine," Harry replied.

"A *what?*" Red yelped.

"A steam-powered traction engine," Harry elaborated and stiffened defensively as she continued, "I know what I'm talking about. My father's driving it."

"Massa Eli had to do it, mister!" Eric put in, determined to set the record straight from the start. He moved protectively to the girl's side and glared at the *big* blond Texan. "The Yankees was holding Miss Harry here so's he'd work ole Pulling Sue for 'em."

"Huh huh!" Dusty grunted, understanding why the girl and the Negro were behaving in such a manner. Many Southrons might regard her statement as treasonable. As always, he was prepared to keep an open mind on the subject. "Maybe you'd best tell me all about it, Miss—"

"Cable," the girl introduced. "Harriet Cable—My friends mostly call me 'Harry.'"

"Yes'm. I'm Dusty Fog, these are my cousins, First Lieutenant Red Blaze and Sergeant Major Billy Jack. If you'll let me tend to a couple of things, I'll hear what you have to say."

"Go ahead," Harry authorized.

"Vern, take Miss Cable's man and tend to the horses," Dusty ordered.

"Eric's a free man—" Harry put in.

"That's how he'll be treated, ma'am," Dusty promised. "Did you see anything of the gun, Cousin Red?"

"Nope," the lieutenant replied, as Hassle guided Eric away with the horses. "Doug figures they'd only put the balloon up to make sure there was none of us around before setting up the gun."

"It's likely," Dusty admitted. "The notices weren't to go up until tonight, so they're not likely to open fire before our folks've had time to read them and decide on whether to set General Culver free."

"It ain't like *me* to think miserable," Billy Jack lied. "But they might've heard we've done catched their spy and are aiming to cut loose straight away."

"Hell, yes!" Red spat out. "What'll we do if that happens, Cousin Dusty?"

"Get back as fast as we can, balloon or no balloon," the small Texan replied; but, even as he spoke, he knew that they would arrive far too late to save Camden from being shelled. "Go and ask Doug to come in for a spell and come back with him, Red. Billy Jack, wake Sergeant Major Smalley and get the men ready in case we have to pull out fast."

"Yo!" Red affirmed and Billy Jack echoed with the traditional Cavalry assent to an order.

"There's a log over by my blankets, Miss Cable," Dusty went on, as soon as his subordinates had taken their departure. "It's the best I can offer by way of a seat and we don't have any coffee—"

"I ate and had some before we broke camp this morning," the girl assured him and sensed that he was deeply perturbed by his cousin's news. She walked towards the fallen tree and sat on its trunk. "What do you want to know?"

"Everything that might help me," Dusty requested, squatting on his heels before her.

"Where shall I begin?"

"At the beginning's usually a good place."

"That would be in England, in 'Fifty-Eight," Harry decided. "Poppa had taken me over there on a combined vacation and business trip. It was just after Momma had died—We met most of the men connected with building steam engines of various kinds. Poppa had done some work on that line and believed they had a great future in America. Anyway, we met James Boydell and Charles Burrell, who'd designed a steam traction engine that used what they called 'endless railway shoes' on the wheels. Poppa saw that it wasn't a practical idea—do you want me to tell you why?"

"Likely I wouldn't know what it was all about," Dusty smiled. "But I'll leave that to you, ma'am."

"I could accept 'Harriet' at a pinch," the girl remarked, finding herself growing to like the *big* young captain. "But I'd prefer 'Harry.'"

"Tell me what you like, Harry," Dusty offered.

"Well, without getting too technical, Poppa saw that the Burrell-Boydell idea wouldn't work. Then he got to know William Bray, the chief engineer on what the British call a cross-Channel paddle steamer. It's like a big riverboat that runs between England and France. Mr. Bray had a really good idea for the kind of wheel to use on a traction engine —that's one meant to travel on land, without rails and—"

"I'd an idea it might be," Dusty told her.

"The wheels were based on the paddles of his steamer, except that the blades moved in and out through the rims and gave a firm grip as they turned. Anyway, Poppa felt that it was a real good idea. So when he brought me home, he decided to use the Bray wheels on his own design of machine. You see, he knew that, especially out West, there wouldn't be a regular supply of coal or coke for fuel. So he worked up a system that gave better combustion with wood than any other steam engine offered."

"And he made up this engine that's hauling the big gun around?"

"It wasn't meant for *that!*" Harry protested. "Poppa had heard about the trials held by the military in England. In May, we'd seen a Bray Patent Traction Engine haul *three* 68-pounder cannons from Woolwich Arsenal to Plumpstead Common, up and down some pretty steep slopes. That was around *twenty* tons. Pulling Sue, our first successful machine, can equal that with wood for fuel and Big Minnie, the second, is even more powerful. Pulling Sue can average a speed of three miles per hour, Dusty. And keep it up for hour after hour, day after day."

"And that's what the Yankees are using," Dusty said quietly.

"Poppa didn't intend his machines to be used for war!" Harry insisted. "If he had, he could easily have made them back East, where he'd've had better facilities and could probably have got financial backing. Especially when it became certain that there must be the war. So he came home to Cable Grange and built them there. He tried to keep their existence a secret, so neither side would benefit from them but they would be ready to help with the re-building once there was peace."

"It didn't work out that way," Dusty drawled, seeing the distress and anguish on the girl's pretty face. It was re-placed by a flicker of anger at his comment.

"It didn't!" Harry conceded bitterly. "Just before the War, while we were in New York buying some equipment, Poppa met Monica Freer. He'd been lonely since Momma's death and—well, Monica's a beautiful woman and, when she's a mind, she can charm a bird down from a tree. They got married and we all went back home. Monica never liked the idea of living out in what she regarded as the frontier and was always wanting Poppa to move back East. Then the War came. Poppa was determined not to let his machines be used for military purposes, which is why we never entertained members of the Confederate States' Army. Then when you started to pull back, Major Lyle and his men arrived. Don't ask me how they knew about Pull-ing Sue and Big Minnie, but they did. No, damn it, why should I lie. I believe Monica had got word to them. Any-way, Lyle arrived. He had brought two companies of sol-diers, all armed with Spencer repeating rifles, and four heavy guns. The thirty-pounder Parrot rifle you're hunting and three Vandenburgs. Do you know what they are?"

"Sure. Multi-barrelled pieces, not long ranged, but real dangerous at close quarters."

"He's using two of the Vandenburgs to cover the bridge from the island and has the other mounted to cover the boats' landing beach, although his men don't guard it too carefully; which's how we escaped. Lyle said that Poppa was to use Pulling Sue to take the Parrot after the Rebels. When Poppa tried to refuse, Lyle said that he would turn us over to his men. What else could Poppa do but obey?"

"Not a whole heap," Dusty admitted. "So Lyle's with the big gun now?"

"No," Harry corrected. "He put the gun and one Company in the hands of his officers and sent them off. He stayed at the Grange, making sure the work he'd demanded was done on Big Minnie."

At that moment, Red returned with Captain Douglas St. John Staunce. Having introduced the girl to the Englishman, Dusty had her go over her story once more. With his companions brought into the picture, he let her continue.

"Lyle's having steel plates put around Big Minnie," Harry warned. "He's going to arm it with two William Rapid Fire cannons that have been captured from the Confederate Army and fix scythes on the wheels to help hold off attackers—"

"The blighter must have met, or heard about, James Cowen," Staunce put in. "He suggested the British Army did the same to the Burrell-Boydell engines, but my father wouldn't have anything to do with such a barbaric idea."

"Lyle doesn't have Sir Arnold's scruples," Harry warned, having met Staunce's father while attending a demonstration of a traction engine's use as an Artillery tractor in England. "He's having the 'improvements' installed, in fact they're nearly completed. Then he's going to use it when the big gun has forced the Confederate Army to come back across the Ouachita. He thinks that Big Minnie will be all that's needed to win the battle."

"An he could be right at that!" Dusty breathed, visualising the effect of such a device against men who would already be outnumbered. "Damn it. More than ever, we've got to get that blasted big gun."

"That won't be easy, with the kind of country that's between us and them, old sport," Staunce warned. "With the balloon up, they'll know we're coming and I'd hate to run into a full company armed with Spencers. Especially when they know we're on our way and can pick their ground."

"You blasted foreigners always wants things too easy," Red scoffed. "And we don't have much choice, except to chance it."

"What's worrying you, Harry?" Dusty inquired, for he could see traces of alarm and perturbation on the girl's face. She had been very helpful, giving them much useful information regarding the strength of the big gun's escort and other matters, but he had suspected that something was disturbing her as she had been doing so. "Something is, I'd say."

"Yes," the girl admitted. "Before Lyle sent Poppa off with Pulling Sue, Mama Lukie—Eric's mother, heard him telling Captain Stabruck that if it looked like the Rebels were going to capture them, Poppa was to be killed to stop him being able to work for the South."

"Whee-dogie!" Red breathed. "Now that's not what I'd call being helpful to us Southron boys."

"Now who's wanting things easy?" Staunce countered, but their expressions told the girl that they were concerned by what they had just heard. "It just means we'll have to play things a mite more carefully, as *you* foreigners say."

"That's for sure," Dusty declared. "Is there anything else you can tell us that might help, Harry?"

"Mama Lukie and Oscar, he's our butler, have told me a few things they've overheard," the girl answered. "Lyle doesn't want to chance losing either Pulling Sue, or the big gun. So he's given orders to Stabruck not to take any chances. If it looks like they might be in danger, they have to pull back to the nearest outfit that has strength enough to protect them."

"That's interesting," Dusty said quietly.

"I've been thinking about that balloon, Dusty," Red remarked. "If it wasn't there, we could likely sneak up on them."

"It *is* there, old thing," Staunce pointed out.

"Why sure," Red replied. "The Company couldn't sneak up on it by day and we'd not get there with enough darkness left to do it, even if they hadn't seen us coming before sun-down, but two, or maybe three of us ought to be able to slip through. Especially if we wore Yankee uniforms."

*"Us?"* Dusty asked.

"I should've said 'me' and a couple more," Red corrected. "You can't go and Doug has to hold those Limey wagon-soldiers' hands so they don't get lost. Which only leaves me."

"Like you say," Dusty drawled, after looking in silence for almost half a minute at his cousin. "That only leaves you. What do you aim to do after you've sneaked up on the balloon?"

"Cut it loose, burn it, burst it, whatever we get the chance to do," Red answered. "I reckon we could get into their camp and do it while most of them's sleeping."

"They could shoot you as spies if they caught you wearing their uniforms," Staunce warned.

"I'm not figuring on letting them catch me," Red countered. "How about it, Dusty? I'll order Vern Hassle and Wilbur Sprigg to volunteer and we'll make a stab at it." Then he looked at the girl. "Thing being, Harry, what're they likely to do to your pappy if we should get rid of their balloon?"

"I don't *think* they'd do anything," the girl decided after a moment's consideration. "They need him to drive Pulling Sue and keep her rolling. But don't let Stabruck lay hands on *you,* Red. He's a soft-shell and hates all Southrons. He'd kill you out of hand and slowly if he caught you, no matter what uniform you're wearing."

"I'll mind it," Red promised cheerfully. "Happen I get to go, that is."

"All right," Dusty sighed. "You're set on going, so I won't stop you."

## CHAPTER TEN

# We've Sure Taken Their Balloon

"Corporal Vernon James Cuthbert Hassle, bearing in mind that I'm your lawful and superior officer and backed by the full and awful powers of the *Manual of Field Regulations*," First Lieutenant Red Blaze whispered, "would you be inclined to say that I maybe talk just a *little* mite too much on occasion?"

"Bearing all that in mind," the ancient corporal replied *sotto voce*, "I'm obliged to come out right truthful and say 'no.' May the Good Lord take pity on me for lying."

"You're a man's'll go far," Red drawled. "Some say the farther the better. Thing being, if I didn't go opening my mouth, we wouldn't be lying here in these blasted bushes and figuring out ways to get ourselves killed or captured—which, according to Harry Cable's likely to come to the same thing."

"You-all-never told me's we could get hurt," the old timer complained, with such querulous bitterness that he might have been speaking the truth. "And, anyways, no matter whether we come this way or with the Company, we'd've had to come in the finish."

"If that's supposed to make me feel happier," Red warned, "it's *not* coming within a good country mile of working."

Peering through the darkness at his youthful companion, Hassle grinned. Since the Battle of Martin's Mill—in which Red had distinguished himself by preventing the destruction of a vitally important bridge—the corporal had come to know him very well and had had no cause to revise the high opinion formed about him. Which might have seemed surprising. To most of Red's elders and supe-

riors, he was a hothead with a penchant for becoming involved in escapades not likely to build up confidence in his
capacity as an officer.

To be truthful, Red did have a happy-go-lucky and
reckless disposition. What Hassle—and Dusty Fog—realized was that when given work of importance, he became
calm, cool and capable of handling it in a responsible manner. Yet, no matter how serious the situation, his sense of
humour was always present. Despite his comments, the
corporal had not shown the slightest hesitation when Red
had asked for his help in the attempt to destroy the Yankees' observation balloon.

Dressed in Union Army's Cavalry kepis, tunics and
breeches—the latter covering their own garments—but
armed and mounted in their usual fashion, Red, Hassle and
the selected private soldier had successfully completed the
first part of their assignment. They had also been granted
ample evidence that there was no other way in which the
destruction of the balloon could be accomplished. It had
been in the air until nightfall and a body of men the size of
Company "C" and the mountain battery could not have
escaped being detected by the observer.

Making use of techniques developed by Hassle and, to a
lesser extent, Private Wilbur Sprigg, while fighting Indians
in Texas before the War, Red's detail had travelled in cover
as much as possible. At a distance, they would have been
indistinguishable from ordinary Yankee soldiers, but they
had not wished to be seen if it could be avoided. Apparently they had been successful, for they had arrived in the
vicinity of their objective without having been intercepted.

Night had fallen by the time the trio had decided that
they dare not risk riding any closer. So, leaving the dis-
gruntled and reluctant Sprigg to keep the horses quiet, Red
and Hassle had completed the journey on foot. They had
wanted to discover what they were up against. On completing his examination, Red had concluded that their task
would be anything but a sinecure. Nor had the youngster
—usually an optimist—ever tried to delude himself and
his companions that it would be.

The Yankees had established themselves in a large hollow about two miles north of the Ouachita River. Apparently they were not unduly concerned about the danger of their position being located, for the bottom of the depression was illuminated by a big fire and several cressets. The hollow was roughly circular and, wishing to prevent their scent being carried to and alarming the enemies' horses, Red and Hassle were concealed among some bushes on the southern side. Looking down, Red took in various details and drew conclusions from them.

The soldiers seemed to be a curious mixture of Cavalry, Infantry and Artillery. Their clothing suggested horsesoldiers, but the long Spencer repeating rifles stacked in pyramidal piles outside the enlisted men's pup-tents were more like Infantry weapons; yet their tunics' facings and breeches' stripes implied that they served in the Artillery. One thing they had in common was an air of tough, hard brutality. According to Harry, both of Lyle's Companies had been recruited from a New York district's gang. The captain and two lieutenants bore traces of mean, vicious and unscrupulous natures and Harry Cable's comments on them had been pungent in the extreme. Having looked the three over, Red was inclined to believe that the girl had been speaking the truth.

Harry's father—who conveyed an impression of strength and intelligence—sat apart from the soldiers, accompanied by the two Negroes who served as the crew of the traction engine. Eli Cable had greying hair, a moustache of considerable proportions, and wore the kind of peaked hat, blue frock coat, trousers and Wellington-leg boots one would more expect to see on a riverboat's captain than the driver of a land machine.

As Cable's party sat near Pulling Sue, Red studied it next. It was a massive piece of machinery, parked on the western side of the camp. On a platform ahead of the boiler and engine was a steering wheel such as might have graced a small paddle steamer and other controls. The chimney was tall and narrow, its top opening out like the head of a lily. From his position, Red could only make out that the rear wheels were almost twice as large as those at the front. He failed to detect the features which Harry had claimed

made Pulling Sue such an effective weight hauler. A four
wheeled trailer, loaded with logs, was hitched to the rear of
the machine in the manner of a railroad engine's fuel tender.

Next Red's attention went to the centre of the hollow.
There stood the big gun, a Parrot 30-Pounder rifle mounted
on a siege carriage, long tube already pointing so that it
could start hurling death and destruction across the river
into the defenceless town of Camden. Never had the
youngster seen such a huge weapon. Neither side in Arkansas had previously possessed siege or garrison Artillery
pieces, their largest weapons being twelve-pounder "Napoleons." So the cannons with which Red was familiar
seemed almost diminutive and puny in comparison with the
greater bulk of the big gun. Its caisson, holding the ammunition supply in three large chests, was secured to the back
of the traction engine's tender.

While Pulling Sue hauled the Parrot and its caisson, the
Yankee party used a number of horses. These stood on
picket lines at the northern side, so that the big gun would
be firing away from them. The majority were the soldiers'
mounts, but there appeared to be a number more suitable to
harness and heavy draught work.

Although the big gun, Pulling Sue, the men and the
horses were of interest to Red, he saved his greatest consideration for the balloon. It was on the east of the camp
and clearly ready for operation. The huge round silk bag
was inflated to such a degree that it tugged against the four
tethering ropes which passed from the corners of the
wicker basket to pegs sunk deep into the ground. The main
anchor cable ran from a hand winch, which was underneath, to pass through the bottom of the basket and be
secured on the inside.

Near by stood two large carts, each with what looked
like an enormous wooden crate on it. Thick hose pipes ran
from the tops of the boxes to metal containers on the
ground. From what Douglas Staunce had said, that would
be the equipment for producing hydrogen gas to fill the
balloon.

"What do you reckon, Vern?" Red inquired, at the conclusion of his scrutiny. He knew the value of requesting advice from an older, more experienced man and was willing to act upon it. "Can we get through?"

"That depends on the sentries," answered the corporal. "We can't say how they'll carry on once the officers 'n' non-coms are in bed. From the look of 'em, they won't be too eager to do their duty."

"Let's hope they're not," Red drawled. "Cousin Dusty'll be madder than a boiled owl happen he gets here and we've been killed instead of destroying that blasted balloon."

"Sure wouldn't want to get the cap'n riled," Hassle admitted. "Was I you, Mr. Blaze, I'd grab me some sleep."

"You get some," Red answered. "I'll take the first watch."

"It ain't worth arguing about," Hassle declared, flipping open the blanket which he had brought from the horses. "Give me a shake at midnight."

"I'll do that," Red promised and took the hacksaw, borrowed from the mountain battery, from his own blanket. Before he had draped the blanket across his shoulders, his companion lay asleep.

Time dragged by on leaden feet. Red kept watch on the camp, selecting a route by which they could pass through the tents and reach the balloon. The sides of the hollow offered too little cover for them to have an easy job. Straight in front of them were the soldiers' pup-tents, with a larger wall-tent for the officers situated between them and Pulling Sue. From all appearances, Cable and his Negroes had to bed down alongside the machine and make do with one pup-tent. After they had retired for the night, a sentry armed with a Spencer rifle started to patrol around their quarters and the traction engine. Another performed a similar service at the balloon and its equipment. One more was over by the picket line. They appeared to be all the guards considered necessary, for no more were in evidence after the rest of the party had retired to their beds.

Just before midnight, as Red was reaching to shake the corporal, he woke up. There was no slow and noisy transition from sleep to awake. With the youngster's hand almost touching his shoulder, the corporal stirred and sat up. Already very tired, Red needed no encouragement to stretch out and close his eyes.

Wrapped in his blanket, Red lay dreaming of attacking the balloon in a wild cavalry charge. Suddenly something descended on his face and covered his mouth. He woke up, trying to struggle.

"Easy, Mr. Blaze!" came Hassle's low-spoken warning. "It'll be sun-up soon." He removed the hand from Red's face, continuing, "Sorry about that, but I didn't want to chance you making any noise when I woke you."

"That's all right, Vern," Red replied, shaking himself from the clutches of the blanket. "I just hope you've not been cleaning out your horse's butt end. What's doing?"

"Nothing so much," the corporal answered, in just too casual a tone but Red was not yet sufficiently awake to notice that. "Still only three sentries out, but they've been a mite more eager than I figured on. They've kept the fire and the cressets going, dang 'em."

"We wouldn't want things *too* easy, now would we?" Red grinned, looking for the sentries.

"*I* would." Hassle declared. "Reckon it's time we got moving, Mr. Blaze."

"Where're those blasted sentries at now?" Red demanded, standing up.

"One's with the hosses, t'other over by Mr. Cable's tent and last 'n's down by the wagons near the balloon."

"I'm damned if I can see the first and last. But the middle bastard's there all right. Lead the way, Vern. I'd rather you got shot than me, I'm younger and've got longer to go."

"Sure does me good to know I'm under an officer's thinks about me welfare," Hassle commented, taking up the hacksaw. "Happen it's all right with you, Mr. Blaze, we'll sort of sneak around the side a ways and come down back of them balloon wagons."

Leaving their blankets behind, Red and Hassle advanced cautiously along the slope. Once clear of the bushes, they still continued to test the ground with each foot before setting it down and making sure that there was nothing underneath that might snap, or roll. In that way, they proceeded silently and apparently without disturbing the sentry who was continuing to prowl around the pup-tent and traction engine. Nor did either of the remaining, unaccounted-for soldiers raise an alarm to show that they were aware of the Texans' presence.

Red was in a state of tension, but not sufficiently to make him grow careless. All too well he realized their peril and fully understood the penalty for failure. If the balloon went into the air at dawn, Company "C" would be spotted approaching and met by volleys of fire from seven-shot repeating rifles. Not only that. The big gun would be free to bombard the helpless citizens of Camden.

Step by step, searching for the first sign of the sentry walking his beat, Red drew closer to the two flat-topped wagons with their big, crate-like loads. At his side, Hassle moved in just as careful silence and scanned the camp with eyes which the years had not dimmed to any great extent.

At first, due to the angle at which he was approaching, Red could not see into the gap between the wagons. Nor could he locate the sentry. When he reached a position from which he could look between them, he received something of a shock.

The sentry was sitting, apparently asleep, with his back resting against the rear of the right side vehicle.

Coming to a halt, the youngster turned the palm of his right hand outwards. He closed his fingers about the wooden, forward-pointing handle of the off side Army Colt. Before he could draw the weapon, Hassle's hand came over to rest lightly on his sleeve.

"Leave him be, Mr. Blaze," the corporal advised in a whisper. "He won't bother us none."

"How come?" Red wanted to know in no louder tones.

"I drifted down this ways while you was asleep, just after they'd changed the guard. Couldn't get the bastard by Mr. Cable's tent, but the other two're wolf-bait. After I'd got this'n, I couldn't see to the balloon without fixing him by the picket line's wagon."

"Likely not," Red grunted. "Why didn't you tell me?"

"I was fixing to until you said for me to get shot afore

you did," grinned Hassle. "Then I figured I'd allow you to find out for yourself."

"*Gracias!*" Red hissed. "Let's see if we can do what we've come for."

Circling the wagons, the Texans halted in the shadows and surveyed the situation. Due to the danger of fire, none of the cressets were too close to the balloon. However, they still threw an uncomfortable amount of light over the area in which Red and Hassle would have to carry out their attempt.

"What do you reckon?" Hassle asked, watching the sentry walking along in front of Cable's tent.

"Let him start going around the machine," Red replied. "Then we'll head over there and take a look."

Following the youngster's suggestion, he and Hassle darted to their objective. The great dome of the balloon towered over them. Bending, they found that the basket had been dragged down almost on to the winch. The gap between them was too small to allow Red or Hassle to use the hacksaw. Gripping the side of the basket, Red hauled himself up and looked in. Several sand-filled ballast sacks hung on hooks around the outer edges. Inside was a couple of chairs and a small table which held a telegraphist's transmission key. None of these items interested Red as much as the sight of the cable coming through the centre of the floor to be secured around a cross bar.

"If we stay out here much longer, we'll be seen for sure," Hassle warned.

"I know," Red replied. "Let's get in. While you're sawing the main rope, I'll cut all but one of the others. Then we'll jump out, cut the last and get the hell away. The balloon'll go up and there'll be no way the Yankees can stop it drifting away."

Agreeing that the idea appeared sound, Hassle climbed nimbly into the basket. Red followed him, crouching below the wicker-work edge. Swiftly the corporal set to work with the saw. Carefully Red rose and, leaning over the side of the basket, used his Russel-Barlow pocket-knife to sever the first of the anchor ropes. As he worked, he kept watch on the traction engine and the Cable's tent.

Clearly the sentry was not hurrying, for Red had released three of the ropes before there was any sign of him.

"She's cut, Mr. Bl—!" Hassle began.

Released from the stabilizing influence of the main cable the balloon started to lift. Held by only one anchor rope, the basket tilted noticeably at the moment the sentry chose to come around the side of Cable's tent. Dropping his knife, Red caught hold of the side. However, he knew that any hope of remaining undetected had ended.

"What the he—!" the sentry commenced, staring at the balloon. Then he began to run forward, unslinging his Spencer. "Who's in that basket?"

Sliding to the lower side, Red twisted the right hand Colt from its holster. Even as the Yankee started to line the rifle, the youngster sighted and cut loose. Struck in the chest, the soldier spun around and fell.

"That does it!" Hassle growled, dropping the hacksaw and straightening up.

Shouts of alarm rang out and men started to erupt from the tents. Sword in hand, a Yankee officer dashed forward to try to prevent the Texans releasing the balloon. Leaning over the edge of the basket, Red placed the muzzle of his Colt against the last anchor rope. He squeezed the trigger and the .44 bullet ripped through the strands. Instantly, the balloon began to rise.

Increasing his speed, the officer prepared to leap and grab the basket. Corporal Hassle snatched one of the sand-filled ballast sacks from its hook and flung it down. Struck on the head, the Yankee dropped his sword and fell as if he had been pole-axed. The balloon continued to ascend, carrying the Texans into the safety of the night-blackened sky.

"Well," Red said, returning the Colt to its holster. "We've sure taken their balloon away from them."

"Looks that way," admitted the old corporal. "There's but one lil thing bothering me, Mr. Blaze. Ain't nothing *too* much, mind, but how do we get the son-of-a-bitching thing down again."

"You know something, Vern?" Red drawled. "I was just

wondering about that myself." He paused, then stared to the east and went on, "Tell Wilbur, in Comanch' to get the hell back to the company and say we've got the balloon."

"I wouldn't know how to say 'balloon' in *Nemenuh,*"* Hassle warned. "But here goes the rest."

During their assignment at the Battle of Martin's Mill, Red and Hassle had used a similar method of preventing the enemy from understanding their instructions to the rest of the detail. The old timer had given his orders in the *Tanima*—Liver Eaters—band's dialect, knowing that there would be less chance of a Yankee understanding it than if he had used his second language Spanish.

As Sprigg's voice faintly acknowledged Hassle's words, the balloon continued to rise.

Although the Yankee soldiers were snatching up their rifles, consternation and considerable confusion delayed them. Before they could take aim, their target had passed beyond their range of vision.

"Ain't wanting to look nosey, Mr. Blaze," Hassle remarked. "But I'd admire to know what you're aiming to do now."

"Wind's still blowing south, what there is of it," Red answered. "So it's pushing us in the right direction."

"Trouble being, the direction we're going's *up*," Hassle pointed out.

"From what Doug Staunce told me, him having done some of this ballooning, it'll only go so high afore it can't lift the weight any more. Only I don't know how high this thing's set to go. Anyways, Doug allows that all a man has to do is pull a rope that's hanging from the bag and it lets the gas out. Then the damned thing stops going any higher."

"Could be it starts going lower—*fast,*" the corporal warned.

"Like you say, *fast,*" Red conceded and looked to where the eastern horizon was growing lighter. "I don't know

---

* Nemenuh: "The People," the Comanche Nation's name for themselves.

what you reckon, but I'm for waiting until we can see what we're at afore we start to try letting the gas out."

"I wouldn't have it any other way," Hassle declared.

Fortunately for the Texans, the wind was not blowing hard. While the basket shook and swayed, its motion was insufficient to cause them any serious discomfort. Gradually daylight came and they could see the land far below them. Not only land, but a river and houses.

"That's Camden!" Red breathed and looked upwards. A length of cord hung from the bottom of the bag and was fastened to one of the basket's ropes. Gingerly he reached out and gave the cord a tug. There was a hissing sound and he stopped pulling. The noise ended.

"Just like Doug said," the youngster told Hassle, who had been watching with considerable interest. "When you pull it, the gas comes out, when you stop there's a spring or something closes the hole."

"What if you're going down too fast?" Hassle wanted to know, as Red once more drew on the cord and allowed hydrogen to leak from the silken bag.

"You start throwing the bags of sand over," Red replied.

Despite the youngster's apparently casual attitude, he was watching and listening to the deflation of the bag and trying to control the rate of descent. Hassle too was looking upwards and neither of them noticed in which direction they were being carried. If they had, they would have observed that they were approaching the Texas Light Cavalry's camp. What was more, in preparation for moving across the river if Company "C" should fail to prevent the bombardment of Camden, the regiment had already formed up by Companies. The men sat their horses with the backs to the rapidly sinking balloon.

"What the hell!" Hassle yelped, looking down at last and realizing what was happening.

By that time, it was too late for Red or Hassle to prevent the balloon from completing its descent. A man looked around, then yelled and pointed. Others turned, staring at the object which came cruising towards them. Next moment, the entire parade was disintegrated. Men spurred their horses out of the balloon's path. Others rode to get clear of the ones who had fled.

The basket struck the ground, bounced and dragged as the hydrogen continued to leave the bag. However, it was still carried onwards by its momentum. Luckily, it was only travelling very slowly when it tipped over and pitched out its occupants.

Sprawled on the ground, Red and Hassle stared about them at the devastation they had created.

"Well," the youngster said. "We've got the blasted thing down."

"Why sure," Hassle agreed and nodded to where a red-faced, furious-looking Colonel Blaze was galloping in their direction. "Know something, Mr. Blaze? I wouldn't give much for your chances of making captain and I don't reckon I'll ever get to be a sergeant."

"I should hope not," Red answered with some feeling. "We can get ourselves into enough damned fuss as we are."

## CHAPTER ELEVEN

# Kill Cable

"Good for Dusty!" Captain Douglas Staunce enthused, springing from his horse agilely despite the Light Artillery sabre which dangled from the slings at the left of his weapon belt and counter-balanced the Army Colt in the close-topped official pattern holster on the right. "He was right about the way they would come."

"Yes, sir," agreed Sergeant Major Smalley, remaining mounted and peering through the trees towards the bottom of the wide valley. "Permission to set up and make ready, sir?"

"Go ahead," Staunce confirmed, continuing to look at and feel admiration over the visible proof of Captain Dusty Fog's astute tactical reasoning. "Make sure that the men don't show themselves and that they know where Captain Fog and his detail are hiding."

Once Red Blaze had gathered his information regarding the balloon and had set off with his two-man detail the previous afternoon, Dusty and Staunce had held a council of war. Their work had been simplified by the fact that the small Texan had recently carried out a long and thorough reconnaissance in the area. He also possessed a range-bred Texan's capacity for remembering terrain after having once traversed it. So his recollections of the vicinity had made up for any possible deficiencies in the large-scale maps which General Hardin had caused to be produced.

Harriet Cable had been called upon to repeat all that she had learned about the big gun and the composition of its escort, particularly about the nature of the officer in command. Being a shrewd, intelligent girl, her comments had been constructive and very helpful. She had told how Captain Stabruck had received orders to run for safety if there should be any danger of the Parrot being captured or destroyed by the Confederate States' Army. In her opinion, he would be only too willing to carry out that order for he was more vicious than courageous.

Trying to put himself into Stabruck's position, after listening to Hardy's unflattering summation of the other's character, Dusty had formed certain conclusions. Red's attempt to destroy the balloon, whether successful or not, would have served as a warning that the Southrons were aware of its connection with the big gun. So, particularly if Red should be fortunate enough to achieve his intentions, Stabruck would assume that the Parrot was in grave peril. In all probability, the Yankee officer would not delay in starting to make good his escape. Harry had stated that she believed the small Texan was thinking on the right lines.

The next question had been where Stabruck would look for the big gun's protection.

While the nearest Union troops were a detachment on the northern bank of the Ouachita River, covering the approaches to the town of Camden, Dusty had doubted if Stabruck would go there. There was only one company each of Infantry and Cavalry, acting as support for two batteries of "Napoleons." They would hardly make an adequate defence against an attack in force and would be far too accessible when one was launched. So Stabruck would go instead to the headquarters of the 6th "New Jersey" Dragoons, probably the best and most efficient Yankee regiment in Arkansas.

Having reached that point, the small Texan and the Englishman had started to consider ways in which they might prevent the big gun and its escort from escaping. Although Dusty had suggested the valley into which Staunce was now looking, they had regretfully concluded that they could not move out immediately. Nor could they leave their attempt until the following night. That meant they would be compelled to carry out their work in daylight.

Except for one detail, Dusty and—more particularly—Staunce would have been content to operate by the light of day. It would permit the howitzers to be aimed with greater ease and so produce better results. There was, however, one vital point which they could not overlook.

The threat to Eli Cable's life.

Apart from the engineer being with the Yankees, it would have been an easy matter for the howitzers to shell the big gun out of existence while the Texans held back the escort.

Harry had appreciated the difficulties created by her father's presence amongst the enemy. However, she had stated her belief that he would prefer to take his chances rather than continue to be a party to the murderous work being carried out by Stabruck.

Bearing in mind the danger faced by Cable, Dusty had suggested a place and the means of making the attack. The plan was based upon his conclusions of the route which Stabruck would take if making for the Dragoons' main camp. It would offer Cable a measure of protection, but also placed Dusty and several members of his Company in grave danger.

Staunce smiled as he thought of the response to Dusty's call for volunteers. Every member of Company "C" had immediately offered his services and, despite having been warned of the risks involved, the ten men he had selected were still as ready to play their parts.

Allowing the enlisted men to rest for the remainder of the day, Dusty and Staunce had continued to develop their arrangements. During the late afternoon, Kiowa Cotton had returned. He was a puzzled man, having found the tracks made by the big gun and its escort without discovering evidence that it was being drawn with a team of horses. Dusty had enlightened his sergeant on the reason for this phenomenon, then had ordered him to grab some sleep. When the Company and battery had moved out after sundown, Kiowa was once more roaming ahead as its scout.

On reaching the valley, Dusty and Staunce had decided that it would suit their needs. There was some work to be carried out, but time had permitted them to make all their arrangements before the enemy had put in an appearance.

Although the bottom of the valley was level and comparatively unobstructed, its sides rose fairly gently and bore a scattered coating of trees, bushes and rocks which became fairly close woodland at the tops. Set up among the trees, Staunce's four howitzers would not be too obvious to anybody passing below but had a good field of fire. They would be shooting from a distance of about half a mile and had need to be accurate. While the main body of Company "C" were hiding with their horses in the woods on the opposite rim, Dusty and his detail had concealed themselves carefully close to the bottom. They were on foot and covered by foliage or other means to prevent themselves from being detected, but leaving them free to appear quickly when the time came.

They were also very close to the area into which the howitzers would be hurling shells!

Before resuming his scrutiny of the enemy, Staunce glanced around to ensure himself that his men were working as swiftly as possible. All was going as he wished. Not that he had expected to find otherwise from his battery's well-trained veterans.

Due to the nature of the terrain they had to traverse, the battery had not been able to move the howitzers limbered for draught. Instead, each piece was carried split into its major components. The tube and the shafts to be used when limbered for draught were on one pack horse, the wheels and carriage on another. Nor had the ammunition been brought in a light weight "prairie cart." Instead it was carried—a pair to a horse—in eight-round boxes.

Each crew was rapidly re-assembling its piece, working without the need for orders or close supervision. Other members of the battery were off-loading and opening the ammunition boxes, to expose the waiting fixed rounds* of various kinds ready for use.

Satisfied that all was well with his side of the affair, Staunce raised a pair of field glasses. Although he knew the positions occupied by Dusty's detail he could not locate any of them as he looked downwards. From there, he made sure that Sergeant Major Billy Jack was holding the remainder of the Texans in their places of concealment.

---

*Fixed round: one with the firing charge attached to the shot.

Changing the direction of the field glasses, Staunce studied the approaching Yankees. From all appearances, they were not expecting trouble. No advance guard preceded the party, nor were there any out-riders on the flanks. That was all to the Southrons' advantage.

A captain and two lieutenants—one of whose head was swathed in bandages—formed an arrowhead in front of the column. Behind them—with Eli Cable standing at the steering wheel on the control platform and his Negro helpers feeding the furnace—Pulling Sue hauled the heavy burden with greater ease than any manageable team of horses could have achieved. Next came the escort. Apart from the first sergeant and sergeant in the lead, who had Spencer carbines dangling from leather carbine slings, the enlisted men were carrying their rifles suspended across their shoulders. The balloon's two supply wagons brought up the rear.

Briefly, Staunce wondered what had happened to Red Blaze. None of the redhead's party had rejoined the main body. However, the fact that the balloon had not been put into the air that morning and that the big gun was being moved away from its intended victims implied that something had been accomplished by the three Texans. Staunce wished that he could find something to suggest that Red had escaped after completing the assignment. The Englishman was equally aware that Dusty was deeply concerned regarding the welfare of his Cousin Red.

"Battery mounted and ready, sir," Sergeant Major Smalley reported, returning on foot to his officer.

"Aim for the main body of the escort," Staunce replied.

"Solid ball, shell, or spherical case, sir?" Smalley inquired.

For a moment, Staunce did not reply. Solid ball would not serve their purpose, being intended for battering holes in objects like walls. Nor was shell, which exploded on arrival provided its fuse had been set correctly, entirely what was required. That left spherical case; which also detonated, but sprayed out seventy-eight musket balls. While the balls were ideal for use against a body of men, they flew indiscriminately and would be dangerous to anybody in their immediate vicinity.

Dusty and his volunteers would be within the range of the balls.

"Spherical case," Staunce finally stated, reaching the decision reluctantly but making it.

"With respect, sir," Smalley warned, "there's not much margin for error."

"Captain Fog and his men accepted *that* when they took up their positions," Staunce replied. "They're game to take their chances and we'll have to hope for the best."

"Yes, sir," Smalley answered.

Both Staunce and the sergeant major were aware of the desperate risks to which Dusty's detail must be exposed in the hope of minimizing the danger to Eli Cable. The smooth bores and round balls of the little howitzers did not make for extreme accuracy, particularly when using spherical case. There were too many unpredictable factors involved for Staunce to have been able to offer his companions complete safety once his battery opened fire.

Crouching behind a rock that was closer to the valley's bottom than the positions of his men, Dusty Fog watched the Yankees drawing nearer. An uprooted bush was placed as naturally as possible above him and its foliage had not yet withered sufficiently to betray him. So far, none of the Yankees appeared to have located any part of the ambush. That was not surprising. There had been considerable effort put into selecting and—although the word had not yet come into general usage—camouflaging the hiding places of his detail. Every man whom he had picked was a veteran Indian fighter and had learned the value of remaining practically motionless at such moments.

Like Staunce, Dusty was deeply concerned over his cousin's fate. To divert his thoughts from how Red Blaze might be faring, the small Texan studied Stabruck and wondered what the Yankee captain was pondering upon.

Riding in the lead of his command, Captain Arthur Stabruck scowled continuously to his front. He slouched morosely on his saddle, ignoring his two lieutenants. All too well he could guess what they were thinking. That it had been his disobedience of orders which was causing their withdrawal and had lost them a valuable observation balloon. So he was trying to decide how he might exculpate himself, or turn the blame elsewhere, when called upon— as he was sure to be—to explain why he had deviated so far from his original orders.

In the first place, Stabruck had merely been dispatched to make a long tour of various outfits, so as to display the hauling powers of the traction engine. It had been drawing its tender, two ammunition caissons and the Parrot rifle. Lyle's idea had been to impress the various regiments' commanding officers and gain their backing for the rest of his scheme.

While travelling down the trail from Malvern to the river opposite Arkadelphia, one of the caissons had broken a wheel. Intending to pass the time while letting his men attempt repairs, Stabruck had ordered the balloon sent up. When the lieutenant who acted as observer had reported a large number of Rebel officers entering a building in Arkadelphia, Stabruck had decided to show initiative. So he had ordered the bombardment. Although he had failed to create the havoc he had hoped among the enemy's officers, he had done considerable damage to a number of buildings before being ordered—by the commanding officer of the detachment covering the approaches to the town—to stop the indiscriminate shelling.

However, the sending of the Rebels' cavalry company —seen and reported by the observer in the balloon—had allowed Stabruck to avoid being called to account for his behaviour. Using the information, he had set up an ambush and driven off his attackers with heavy losses. After which, he had turned off the trail and headed east parallel to the Ouachita River.

A chance meeting with a friend who was a member of the United States Secret Service had presented Stabruck with what had seemed—at the time—an ideal opportunity to gain personal acclaim and to win an important, influential supporter. Learning that his friend had a contact on the other side of the river, he had caused the printer of the Fordyce, Dallas County, newspaper to produce the warning notices. By doing so, he had hoped to secure General Culver's release from captivity.

With the balloon stolen, Stabruck had been fully aware of the danger. So he had set his men immediately to breaking camp. While he was heading for the main body of the 6th "New Jersey" Dragoons, he had not sent a messenger with word of his coming so that he might have been granted a larger escort.

There had been two reasons for the omission.

Firstly: if the Rebels had not sent a force to destroy the Parrot, Stabruck would have been regarded as a cowardly alarmist who had panicked and fled without any cause to do so.

Secondly: the reaction of the detachment's commanding officer had warned him that his activities might not receive a favourable reaction; especially when he had failed to achieve his purpose.

So Stabruck intended to arrive at the Dragoons' camp, as if on the mission for which he had been dispatched. If he should be questioned about the bombardment of Arkadelphia, he would claim he had been trying to wipe out a large number of Confederate senior officers.

Once certain that there was no danger, Stabruck could return to Nimrod Lake and rejoin Lyle. Later, after a new commanding general had been appointed, they could put up their idea to force the Confederate States' Army to return across the Ouachita River. Having brought about the full scale confrontation, they could use the second of Cable's machines to ensure a Northern victory.

Thinking about the latter point, Stabruck saw something which he might use as an excuse for revising Lyle's plan. He would claim that he had hoped to secure Culver's freedom so that the confrontation and defeat of the Rebels could be accomplished without delay.

While the Union captain and his men rode onwards along the bottom of the valley, completely oblivious of their peril, the crews of the four howitzers had made everything ready to open fire.

Each chief-of-piece had aligned his barrel and adjusted its elevation to the correct five degrees angle for the distance over which it would be firing. The fuses had been cut so that—in theory at any rate—they would cause the burster charges to detonate when the cases were a few feet above the mass of Yankee horsemen; and the fixed rounds were rammed fully home.

Everything was now waiting for Staunce to give the word of command.

Moving behind his battery, the English captain took up a position between the Numbers Two and Three howitzers. He stared into the valley, watching the traction engine drawing level with the small Texan's position.

"Good luck, Dusty!" Staunce breathed, then raised his voice. "Get set, men. Ready! Fire!"

On their officer's order, four hands tugged sharply at the firing lanyards. Even as the quartet of howitzers bellowed in what came as practically a single sound, Smalley stared towards the other side of the valley and waved his right hand over his head.

Sitting his horse at the top of the second slope, Sergeant Major Billy Jack was able to watch the battery's preparations. Receiving Smalley's signal, the gangling Texan swung his doleful features towards the waiting men of Company "C."

"Let's go and get ourselves killed," Billy Jack suggested, sounding as if he believed that it was certain to happen. "Company, forward at a walk. Yo!"

With that, the sergeant major started his mount moving. The rest of the Company, formed into a single line, followed him. When the spherical case shells exploded, he increased the pace and they were soon galloping recklessly down the slope.

From his place, Dusty had been unable to make out what was happening on either rim. However, he knew that the howitzers would speak as soon as the traction engine was passing his position. Slowly it rolled level, but he refrained from moving. To appear prematurely might spoil all his carefully laid plans.

The attack took Stabruck and his men completely by surprise. Curving through the air, the shells were descending towards their targets before the bellows of the howitzers reached the bottom of the valley. One exploded too high to be very effective, but the other three's fuses burned with greater accuracy. The triple eruption of burned powder smoke were accompanied by musket balls scattering in all directions.

Men and horses were struck by the balls. The animals which had not been hit displayed alarm and fright at the sudden noises. In a moment, the four lines of blue-clad riders were disrupted and thrown into utter confusion.

Before Dusty could start to rise, he felt something strike the bush which was covering him and a musket ball fanned his cheek in passing. Ignoring the thought of how close he had come to being struck by one of his companions' missiles, he hurled aside the foliage and thrust himself erect.

"Yeeah! Texas Light!" Dusty bellowed, hands flashing down and across to draw the matched Army Colts.

The remainder of the volunteers for the assignment also sprang into view. Each man held the weapon—or weapons—of his choice and they were spaced along the bottom of the slopes.

Twisting on his saddle at the sound of the shells exploding, Stabruck was almost unseated as his horse plunged. He managed to retain his seat and started to rein the animal around.

"Kill Cable!" Stabruck screeched, right hand clawing at the flap of his holster.

Hardly had the words left the Yankee captain's mouth than a bullet, fired by one of Dusty's detail, ripped into his head and toppled him lifeless to the ground. Neither of the lieutenants survived him by many seconds, for the Texans knew the value of depriving their enemies of leadership.

Despite the confusion and pandemonium that raged behind them, Stabruck's first sergeant and the other three-bar heard his order. They also remembered what they had been instructed to do in the event of an attack. Sending their horses plunging forward, they liberated their carbines from the clips of the slings. One of them headed along each side of the traction engine, determined to prevent the engineer from being taken alive by the attacking Rebels.

Hurdling over the rock, Dusty swung up and fired his right-hand Colt. He sent its bullet into the first sergeant's chest. Rocking backwards on the saddle, the Yankee non-com let his carbine fall and slid after it. However, Dusty knew that he could not hope to deal with the second would-be killer.

Being aware of the plans laid for his employer's removal, one of the Negroes acted fast. He thrust the shovel he was holding into the furnace and brought it out again heaped with red hot chunks of wood. Swinging, he hurled them into the sergeant's face. Even as the stricken soldier started to scream, one of Dusty's volunteers shot him in the head.

With many of their horses rearing and pitching wildly, none of the Yankee soldiers were in a condition to make a fight. Some had been thrown off, others found themselves being carried away by their bolting mounts. The remainder, conscious of having their rifles slung in an inaccessible manner, strove to regain control of their mounts and surrender.

Inside five minutes, the incident had ended. The three Union officers and two senior non-coms were all dead, the enlisted men who had not fled stood disarmed. Harry Cable was enfolded in her father's arms and the big gun was in the possession of the Confederate States' Army.

## CHAPTER TWELVE

## He Takes Real Pleasure in Killing

"Sergeant Weather!" Captain Dusty Fog barked, swaggering arrogantly to where the stocky non-com was supervising the captured Union soldiers. "You'll take six men and escort these Yankee bastards to our lines."

"Six men?" Weather repeated, sounding worried and uncertain. "May I suggest that—?"

"The hell you may!" Dusty roared, quivering with well-simulated rage at the sergeant's action. "You'll do as I said."

"With respect, sir," Weather protested, stiffening into a brace. "Last time proved six men can't control so many prisoners."

"Things turned out all right *last* time, and they will *this* time, sergeant," Dusty answered, without looking at the prisoners but conscious that they were hanging on his very word. "You and your men will all have repeaters. Don't hesitate to use them. It's all one to me whether any of these Unionist scum are still alive when you reach the Ouachita."

"But that'd be murd—" Weather commenced.

"You'll take that escort as its sergeant," Dusty interrupted coldly, "or ride in it as a private. It's your choice."

"Yo!" Weather grunted and saluted.

Having listened to the conversation, the prisoners exchanged glances with each other. Six men would not be a large number to act as their escort, so they would have the opportunity to escape. Or might have had, if that damned short-grown captain had not made known his views on the matter. They watched Dusty walk away and Weather approach them. The sergeant looked concerned, alarmed almost, by the orders he had received.

"That captain sounds like a real mean bastard," one of the Yankee corporals remarked.

"You don't know the half of it," Weather replied, grateful for the comment as it allowed him to pass on further information without arousing the Yankees' suspicions. "He's the most cold-blooded bastard I've ever ridden under. He takes real pleasure in killing."

"We've got two of 'em like that," the corporal admitted. "Or did have. You killed one of 'em."

"Was I you fellers," Weather continued, hiding the delight he was feeling at the way the deception was going. "I'd not even look like I was *thinking* about escaping. You'll right soon wish you hadn't if you try it."

"How's that?" demanded another of the blue-clad soldiers.

"We had to do something like this during the withdrawal," Weather explained, sounding so convincing that his audience did not doubt that they were hearing the truth. "He sent off a small escort with a big bunch of prisoners, but followed without them knowing. When the prisoners tried to escape, he brought the rest of the Company down and butchered them all."

Watching the prisoners as he spoke, Weather could read alarm on every face. Having served under two officers who they knew were capable of such an act, the Yankees were willing to believe that Dusty would not hesitate to put it into effect. That had been the reason for the performance. The small Texan hoped that it would persuade the prisoners to co-operate and so make their disposal easier.

Having no wish to be hampered by the captured Yankees, nor the desire to weaken his force by sending them away under an adequate guard, Dusty had arranged the little byplay with Sergeant Weather. If the deception had worked, Weather and his men would have no trouble controlling the prisoners for as long as necessary. What was more, it would be possible to leave them with a suitable impression on another matter.

"Sergeant!" Dusty shouted. "Get those bastards moving. We'll take the big gun with us."

"Yo!" Weather replied. "You heard the captain. Get ready to pull out."

"If they show signs of being ornery, send a rider back for us," Dusty went on. "We'll not be *too* far away."

"*Just* like last time," Weather sighed, looking at the prisoners. "Form up and get moving, or he might not even let you go."

Staunce had joined Dusty and they stood side by side, watching Weather's detail mount up. Forming around the prisoners, who were on foot, the Texans started them moving in a southerly direction.

"A very convincing performance, if I may say so," the Englishman declared, grinning at his companion.

"Feel free to say it," Dusty authorized cheerfully.

"I don't think Sergeant Weather will have much trouble with them," Staunce went on.

"Nope," Dusty agreed. "Just so long as Stormy can keep them moving until nightfall, everything'll be fine. Then he and his men can leave them and join us. Time they've met up with more Yankees, we'll be long gone and, with luck, they'll all figure we've gone back south of the Ouachita."

"Now we'd better go and talk to Mr. Cable," Staunce suggested, feeling as Dusty did that the deception would produce the desired results.

"Why sure," Dusty agreed. "Let's see if we can get him to back our play."

"What if he won't, Dusty?" Staunce inquired.

"I don't know," the small Texan confessed frankly. "Let's hope that he will help, and leave trying to decide what to do next until *after* he's refused."

From what Harriet Cable had told them about Big Minnie, the second and more powerful of her father's machines, Dusty and Staunce had recognized that it posed a very serious threat to the Army of Arkansas and North Texas. More than that, the success of Big Minnie would lead to the production and use of similar traction engines by the Union. The North's industrial capacity would permit them to bring out the machines in a comparatively short time and the Confederate States had nothing with which to counter them. So the young officers had decided that, if they were successful in their attempt to liberate the engineer and capture the big gun, they would also try to destroy the armoured traction engine before it could be put into the field.

Encouraging Harry to talk, partly as a means of taking her mind off the danger which their attack would cause to her father, Dusty and the Englishman had formed a pretty fair estimation of the conditions they would be up against. Possession of the big gun, which Staunce and his men could operate, would be of the greatest assistance. It might make all the difference between success and failure.

Providing, of course, that they could take it to Nimrod Lake.

Everything depended on Eli Cable agreeing to help them.

Harry and her father were sitting together on the control platform of the traction engine, while Eric was talking with the other two Negroes by the still burning furnace. As the two officers approached, the girl and Cable dropped to the ground.

Looking at the approaching pair, Harry sensed what was bringing them. Being shrewd and intelligent she had guessed what had been behind their interest in Big Minnie and curiosity regarding the defences of the island. She was equally aware of the purpose to which they hoped to put Pulling Sue.

Gripping her father's arm with her left hand, Harry looked up at him. From the first moment she had seen that he was safe, she had been deeply disturbed and anxious regarding his reactions to her having deserted her stepmother. She had hated the thought that she must tell her father of Monica's betrayal. Yet, much to her amazement and perturbation, he had not pressed her for information on the point which she had been dreading. Instead, he had merely asked if Monica was in good health and had turned the conversation to the subject of her escape. Harry did not know what to make of that development. It almost seemed that he had known, or suspected, his wife's infidelity; but wished to prevent Harry from realizing that he did so.

"I haven't had the opportunity to thank you gentlemen for saving me," Cable announced, but his tone was wary and his eyes watchful. "I'm most grateful to you for your consideration to Harry as well as to me."

"Think nothing of it, sir," Dusty answered, feeling just a touch uncomfortable. "We couldn't let the Yankees go on shelling our towns."

"And we couldn't let the Yankees continue to use your machines," Staunce went on, understanding his companion's predicament and stepping into the breech. "Either of them."

*"Either* of them?" Cable repeated, although he could guess what had been meant and how the conversation might develop.

"I've told Dusty and Doug what Lyle's planning to do with Big Minnie, poppa," Harry put in.

"We can't let him turn that iron-plated machine loose, sir," Dusty warned. "Either here, or back East."

"Back East?" Cable asked, looking puzzled.

"That'll be the next step," Dusty pointed out. "They'll be figuring to show how well the machine works here in Arkansas, then taking it or the plans and know-how back East, then start making more to smash down the Confederate States."

"It won't stop there, either," Staunce continued. "As soon as the various European military advisers see what a terrible—and effective—weapon it is, they'll all start making or buying them. After which, whoever gets them first will be all set to conquer its neighbours."

"I didn't design my machines to be used for war or killing," Cable sighed. "They were meant to help people, not to take human lives."

"I'd say a whole heap of inventions started out the same way, sir," Dusty answered. "Trouble is, human beings being the way they are, sooner or later somebody figures out a way to use them for fighting or killing."

"That's true," Cable confirmed, looking with renewed interest at the *big* blond Texan and wondering how one so young could have gained such an insight into human frailties. He also compared Dusty with Lyle and Stabruck, not to the Yankee's advantage.

"The thing is, sir," Dusty went on. "As officers in the Confederate States' Army, Doug and I have to try to stop the Yankees using the machines. And we need your help to do it."

"I see," the engineer said softly.

"It's not an easy thing we're asking, sir," Dusty conceded. "We want you to take the big gun to Nimrod Lake for us, so that we can use it to destroy your other machine."

"It will have to be 'destroy,' sir," Staunce continued. "We'll not pretend that we think we can capture it. We couldn't get either of them back to our lines. So we'll have to destroy them both."

"With *my* help," Cable said.

"Yes, sir," Dusty agreed. "We know that can't come easily to you. But they have to be destroyed. With the big gun, we can do it and not lose so many lives. Without it, we're going to have to go in ourselves and there's no easy way to do that. I can't even promise you that you won't be asked to make machines for the South. All I can say is that I'll make General Hardin know how you feel and ask that he helps you to go somewhere that you can go on with your work for peaceful purposes."

"It all depends on you, Mr. Cable," Staunce continued. "If you won't help us, there's no way we can make you."

"Lyle and Stabruck found a way," Cable pointed out.

*"We're* not Lyle and Stabruck," Dusty countered. "If you say 'no,' I'll have some of my men escort you to anywhere you will feel safe."

"And go after Big Minnie anyway?" Cable asked.

"That's what we have to do, sir," Dusty stated.

"I can't let you shell the island," Cable said, looking from one officer to the other. "My—"

"If it's because Monica is still being held there—," Harry began, the words bubbling out then away to nothing as she could not bring herself to utter them.

"That's part of it," Cable confirmed and smiled at his daughter. "I'm not entirely a fool, or blind, Harry."

"You *know* about—?" the girl gasped, a mixture of relief and alarm filling her.

"We'll talk about it later," Cable promised and returned his attention to the two captains. "Mama Lukie, Oscar and all our other people are on the island. They're only Negroes—"

"They're folks, same as everybody else," Dusty interrupted. "And I know how you feel about them. So you've got my word that we won't open fire unless they're going to be safe."

"I'll go with Dusty on that, sir," Staunce declared. "You've my word on it too."

"In that case, gentlemen," Cable said. "I'll help you take the big gun to Nimrod Lake."

"We'd like to get moving as soon as those Yankees are out of sight, sir," Dusty suggested. "If that's all right with you."

"That's easy enough arranged," Cable replied. "We're ready to roll. You certainly frightened them."

"I aimed to," Dusty admitted. "The next thing is to make them think we've blown up the big gun and everything else. Then they'll be more willing to figure we're trailing them along."

"I see you've an extra ammunition chest on the caisson, Mr. Cable," Staunce put in.

"Yes," agreed the engineer. "We started out with two caissons, but one broke a wheel and we left it behind. We'd emptied the other two chests bombarding Arkadelphia."

"Are you figuring on using the big gun's powder charges, Doug," Dusty asked.

"Not if I can avoid it," the Englishman replied. "And I think I can avoid it. The containers are full of hydrogen. It explodes in a very satisfactory way."

How satisfactorily was proven when Staunce blew up the two wagons which had serviced the balloon.

On hearing the massive explosions, although unable to see what had happened, the Yankee prisoners assumed that the big gun and its accessories had been destroyed. They also believed, helped by Sergeant Weather's hints, that

Company "C" and the battery were following at a distance and looking for an excuse to massacre them. So they were willing to go along with Weather's suggestion that they spend the night in an area of woodland. Once there, he warned that he would find himself in serious trouble for circumventing the plans of the evil "Captain Yancy's"—he refused to use Dusty's real name in connection with the bloodthirsty tyrant the young officer had pretended to be. So he and his men intended to desert.

Left to themselves, the Yankees had remained hidden in the woodland for three days. Finally hunger drove them out and they realized that they had been tricked. Long before they could reach the nearest Union troops, there was no way to know in which direction the big gun had been taken. On hearing the prisoners' story, the officer in command assumed that it was already across the Ouachita River and made no attempt to verify his theory.

## CHAPTER THIRTEEN

# I Got Them Here for You

"Cousin Titus!" Eric called, riding from among the bushes and on to the Perryville trail. "I'm right pleasured to have come across you-all."

Bringing his mule to a halt, the tall, lean, sharp-featured Negro stared from Eric to where Captain Douglas Staunce followed him out of the bushes. The Englishman was still armed with his Light Cavalry sabre and Colt revolver, but in every other respect he looked exactly like a captain in the United States' Army. The top of his kepi—which had been brought along as easier than a Burnside hat to carry in concealment—sported the crossed sabres insignia of the Cavalry. The shoulder bars of his short blue "uniform jacket" showed the two pairs of gold bars of a captain.

"Why howdy, Cousin Eric," Titus finally replied, but his attention was mainly directed at Staunce and his sly face showed puzzlement. "That Yankee major's done been madder'n a cat dropped on a hot stove ever since you-all run off. Where've you been at?"

"With Miss Harry, looking for Massa Cable," Eric answered, seeing no point in lying about the reason for his departure. "We've been going from one Yankee camp to another, until we got to some real high up 'n' important officers. They said for me to fetch this gent back with me."

"Who'd he be?" Titus wanted to know.

"Name's Captain Schmidt," Eric supplied, following the line which had been suggested to him by the Englishman. "He's wanting to find out just what's happening on the island."

"I'd've thought you-all, or Miss Harry could've telled

132

him that," Titus commented, still studying Staunce rather than his cousin.

"I have to see for myself," the Englishman barked, adopting the harsh, Teutonic accent which he had used when helping to trick the Union agent, Meats. "These men might not be what they've told you they are."

"You-all reckons's how they might be peckerwoods, mister?" Titus asked.

"They just may be," Staunce lied, deciding that such a response would help bring the desired result. "I've been sent with Eric to find out the truth."

"Which means we can't go across the bridge, like we was regular calling-folks," Eric went on. "So we'd admire to get some help, cousin."

"Such as?" Titus inquired, sounding wary and a little worried.

"Can you fetch us a boat down to the river's mouth after dark, so we can sneak in the back ways?"

"Well, I dunno about that——"

"I don't reckon Mama Lukie'd be any too pleasured happen she heard you wouldn't help us, cousin," Eric remarked and watched the flicker of anxiety and alarm which passed over the other's face. "Especially as doing it wouldn't be hard, nor dangerous, and'd help Massa Cable."

"How d'you mean?" Titus countered, scratching his head dubiously. "'Bout it not being hard or dangerous, I mean."

"Them Yankees, or whatever they be, ain't stopped you fellers going out on the lake catfishing, have they?"

"Well, no. I can't say's they has."

"Then, happen you gets asked, you're going catfishing," Eric explained.

"I reckon I could do that," Titus conceded. "Tell you what. I'll bring a boat down to them willows near the river's mouth just after sundown."

"That'll be real fine, Cousin Titus," Eric enthused, although he felt just a trifle surprised that his kinsman had agreed so easily, even allowing for the power of Mama Lukie's name. "We'll be waiting for you."

After the lanky Negro had set the mule into motion and was riding away, Staunce and Eric returned to the concealment of the bushes. Although Titus had not known, another pair of eyes had been studying him. Watching from a position which had allowed him to keep the trail under observation, although hidden from all but the most careful scrutiny, Kiowa Cotton stood by his big horse. The sergeant had reverted to wearing his Confederate States' uniform and had decided that it would be advisable to remain undetected while Staunce and Eric went out to interview the latter's cousin.

"We've got a boat to take us out to the island after dark," Staunce announced. "I'll go with Eric, but you'd better stay in the background, sergeant. Then, if anything goes wrong, you can let Captain Fog know about it."

"Yo!" Kiowa answered, knowing that the Englishman was suggesting a sensible precaution. Then he looked at the Negro. "You reckon that jasper can be trusted, Eric?"

"I reckon he can," Eric replied, after a moment's thought. "Cousin Titus don't look much and I wouldn't throw dice with him, less'n I'd searched him all over afore we started, but this here's different. He ain't going to go crossing Mama Lukie on anything this important. No darkie ever wants to get a conjure woman like her riled at him."

"That's for sure," Kiowa admitted and concluded that their mission was going much better than he had hoped.

The journey from the valley in which they had captured the big gun had been uneventful; except that Sergeant Weather's detail had successfully slipped away from the prisoners and Wilbur Sprigg had caught up with news of Red Blaze's exploits. The latter had only been a partial relief for Dusty Fog. He had found out that his cousin had not fallen into the Yankees' hands, but wondered how Red's flight in the balloon had ended.

While travelling northwards, the party had avoided being seen by, or meeting with, Union soldiers. There had been a few difficulties, most concerned with negotiating uneven terrain, but nothing had occurred to delay them unduly. The main body was now within one day's travel, at the best speed possible for Pulling Sue and its burden, from Nimrod Lake. Wishing to make contact with the Negroes on the island and, if possible, arrange for them to leave before the big gun was brought on to the scene, it had been decided to send a small detail ahead.

The spin of a coin had decided that Staunce should come, accompanied by Kiowa and Eric. After some discussion, it had been decided that the sergeant should remain clad in Confederate grey. However, Staunce had elected to dress as a member of the Union Army. He had in his possession identity documents to "prove" he was Captain Schmidt, attached to the Adjutant General's Department,* which might come in useful in the event of a meeting with Yankee soldiers. Nor would his British-made sabre be out of place, for many Federal officers owned such weapons.

On reaching the Fourche la Fave River, in the late afternoon, Staunce and his men had intended to find a boat as a means of reaching the island. Before they could do so, the chance meeting with Eric's cousin appeared to have solved that problem for them.

Keeping in concealment amongst the bushes the three men made their way to the point where the river flowed out of the lake. Still remaining in hiding, they examined the island. Using his field glasses, Staunce watched Titus crossing the bridge. At that distance, the captain could tell only a little of what was happening and saw nothing to alarm or make him suspicious. The lanky Negro was stopped by and talked with the Union sentries, but they displayed no signs that he was mentioning the meeting with his cousin. Passing on, Titus went beyond the Englishman's range of vision.

Despite keeping a constant watch until the sun had sunk below the western horizon, Staunce and his companions could see nothing to make them think their presence in the area was known. As the bats started to glide through the air, hunting food above the calm waters of the lake, lights

---

* Supplied to "prove" his identity if challenged during the plan to trap the spy at Stilton Crossing.

began to glow on the island. Cressets were lit, illuminating the bridge and other points, while the windows of the main house and Negroes' dwellings showed that lamps were burning within.

About an hour of darkness dragged slowly by, with the three men watching the island and the waters of the lake for any indication that Titus was keeping his promise.

"It looks like he thought better of it," Staunce commented.

"If he did, Mama Lukie'll make him wish he'd never been born," Eric replied. "She's never liked him, 'cause he wants to be butler instead of Paw."

"Could be we're doing him an unjust," Kiowa put in, staring across the water. "There's a boat coming."

"We'd better keep hidden, just in case he's bringing friends," Staunce suggested, accepting the warning, for he had had numerous examples of the sergeant's exceptionally keen sight and hearing. "I hope you don't mind us mistrusting your cousin, Eric?"

"Can't say's I do," Eric answered. "Fact being, no matter how he says he don't, I know he's scared of Mama Lukie, or I wouldn't trust him either."

A few seconds later, first Eric then Staunce could make out the shape of a large boat moving slowly in their direction. For all their doubts, they soon saw that there was only one man in it. Kiowa faded silently into the darkness before Titus, grunting and gasping with his exertions, brought the bows of the boat into the shallows.

"I'm sorry I wasn't here sooner," the lanky man said, when his cousin and the Englishman walked forward. "Only this here boat's made for two fellers to row and I'm alone."

"It'll be easier going back," Staunce promised and stepped aboard. "Eric will be helping you to row."

"You mean I've got to go back with you?" Titus yelped, sounding alarmed at the prospect.

"Why shouldn't you?" Eric demanded, eyeing his cousin with suspicion.

"Well, I was fixing on going down to Salty Annie's—" Titus answered.

"Shucks, that's no fitten place for a Gawd-fearing, upright young feller like you," Eric interrupted. "Stay put. Like you said, that boat's meant for two fellers to row it."

While Staunce took a seat in the stern, Eric shoved the boat back into deeper water. Boarding it, the young Negro took one of the oars. Reluctantly, Titus helped his cousin to row in the direction of the island. Even in the darkness, Staunce could tell that the lanky man was very nervous. Probably, the captain mused, that was because he lacked Eric's courage and was frightened of the consequences if he should be caught by the soldiers who occupied Cable Grange.

Guided by Eric, the boat swung across the lake and towards the rear of the island. Although the main section of the landing beach was illuminated by a pair of cressets, they were in need of replenishment and threw out little light. Once clear of them, the rest of the shore lay in satisfactory darkness.

Peering between the two Negroes, Staunce sought for any suggestion that they might have been seen. He failed to detect anything to alarm him. If there had been guards assigned to keep watch on the beach, they were not carrying out their duties in an efficient manner. However, Harry had stated that strict attendance to military duties was not a conspicuous virtue among Lyle's soldiers.

Certainly nobody challenged, or gave other indications of being aware of the boat as it ran silently through the gloom and grounded its bows a short distance from the bank. Climbing out, the men made their way cautiously and watchfully ashore.

"This way!" Titus hissed and his voice was throbbing with strain as he darted nervous glances around him. "Mama Lukie said for me to fetch you-all to the workshop."

Without bothering to answer, for it was neither the time nor the place for conversation, Staunce and Eric followed the lanky man towards the big building. Leading the way to a side door near a lean-to which housed the Cables' carriage and other vehicles, Titus let them precede him through it. The interior of the workshop was sparsely lit by a couple of hanging lamps and it appeared to be deserted.

Concluding that Mama Lukie had not yet arrived, Staunce gave his attention to the second of Eli Cable's machines. Few details of its appearance could be seen, for it was encased in a box-like iron structure which hid the engine and control platform. The metal sides were pierced with rifleslits and the Williams Rapid Fire cannons were positioned to fire respectively to the front and the rear. Although the door in the side was open, none of the lamps' light reached beyond it and Staunce could not make out anything of the interior. For all that, he assumed the machine was practically ready to put into operation.

"Where's Mama Lukie?" Eric demanded, turning to his cousin when they were about half way to the machine.

"She'll be along," Titus answered, but his eyes were darting from point to point as if he was expecting somebody to already be present.

"I don't like this, Captain St—" Eric began, returning his gaze to the Englishman.

At that moment, footsteps sounded from the doorway by which the men had entered. They were heavy, hurrying, masculine feet and threw an ominous note into the proceedings. Especially when taken in conjunction with the two figures who jumped from the machine's doorway.

They were dressed in the uniforms of the United States' Artillery!

First out, going to the left, was a big, burly, black bearded sergeant with a heavy sabre in his right fist. Next, moving to the right, came an equally large enlisted man who carried a Spencer rifle and turned its barrel in Staunce's direction.

"I got them here for you, Sergeant Block!" Titus announced, scuttling forward hurriedly.

"You bastard!" Eric shouted and sprang after his cousin.

Bringing up his left hand, Block—who had been promoted to replace the previous sergeant after he had been killed in a quarrel over a card game—thrust Titus to the right. Then he went into a pretty fair lunge with the sabre. Unable to halt, Eric advanced to meet the out-driving point. It pierced his left breast and continued to burst out at the rear. Killed instantly, Eric hung on the blade until Block wrenched it out and allowed him to fall.

Although Titus had been thrust to safety, he came between Staunce and the enlisted man's rifle. Trying to make the most of the chance presented to him, the Englishman flashed his right hand towards the flap of his holster. Just an instant too late, he remembered having heard footsteps coming from behind him. While he had become aware that there was probably another enemy to his rear, the realization, or recollection, had not come quite soon enough.

Having hidden in the lean-to until the men had entered, Private Grilpan was on hand and close enough to prevent the Englishman from drawing a weapon. Darting forward, the soldier swung the butt of his Spencer against the back of Staunce's head.

For a moment, bright lights seemed to burst inside Staunce's skull. Then everything went black for him.

"Oh my Lord!" Titus croaked, staring horrified at the twitching, gory body of his cousin. "You killed him!"

"So what?" Block countered calmly.

"Lordy, lord!" Titus moaned. "I've got to get away from here. Mama Lukie—"

"Shut up, you stupid black bastard!" Block snarled. "Go make sure none of the niggers've heard anything, Dasour. Make sure that bastard's not faking, Gril. I said shut up!" The last words were directed at the whining, clearly terrified Negro. "We'll not let anything happen to you."

"You-all can't stop what she'll do to me!" Titus moaned. No longer did he pretend to have no belief in the powers of the conjure woman. Instead, he was filled with superstitious dread. So much so that he could barely stand, or take his eyes from Eric's corpse. "She'll put a hex on me and I'll—"

"He's alive, Blocky," Grilpan announced, having knelt by Staunce and conducted a perfunctory examination. Unbuckling the officer's waist belt, he dragged it and its weapons free. "That's how Lyle said for us to get him."

"Nobody's heard nothing, Blocky," Dasour called from the door.

"There, you ignorant black bastard!" the sergeant raged at the quivering Negro. "Nobody heard him yell out. So how'll she know what's happened. She reckons this—" He kicked the corpse contemptuously and started to wipe the blood from his sabre on Eric's clothing—"son-of-a-bitch is with the Cable gal."

"She—She'll know!" Titus insisted.

"Listen!" Block snarled, raising the sabre so that its point touched the black throat of the cringing man. "I'll tell you what we'll do. We'll fasten some weights to his legs. Then Dasour'll help you tote him to a boat. You can row him into the lake and drop him over. That way she'll never find out what happened."

"I—I!" Titus began.

"Go and fetch the old whore down to see what we've done to her son," Block growled over his shoulder.

"N—No!" Titus almost screamed, eyes rolling and face wet with perspiration. "I'll do like you say."

"I figured you would," Block sneered. "Lend him a hand, Dasour. Come on, Gril, we'll haul this bastard up to the house."

"What do you reckon Lyle'll do with him, Blocky?" Grilpan inquired as they grasped Staunce by the arms and started to drag him from the workshop.

"I dunno," the sergeant admitted. "But I'm willing to bet on one thing. No matter who he is, nor what he's doing here, he won't leave alive."

"You reckon Lyle'll chance killing him?" Grilpan asked.

"I reckon he might at that," Block confirmed. "He's got him some mighty big ambitions and he's not about to let anybody spoil them."

"Us knowing so much of what's been going on," Grilpan said thoughtfully. "We ought to be able to do pretty well for ourselves after the War."

"I wouldn't count on it," Block warned. "If he offers us anything, we'll take it. But he's one bastard I wouldn't want to try to blackmail."

Being aware of the kind of man the sergeant was, Grilpan felt impressed and revised his views on the hoped-for life of wealthy ease that he had hoped could be obtained from Lyle.

Although Titus was shivering, fear lent him the strength to help carry out Block's orders. His hope that Dasour would not accompany him came about and he wasted no time in rowing his burden away from the island. Once he had reached an area of deep water, he mustered his courage and started to raise the body. Muttering prayers that were incongruous when taken with the evil work he was doing, he tipped his cousin over the side. Watching Eric's body sink, Titus reached for the oars with trembling hands. He had no intention of returning to the island. Instead, he decided that he would make for the shore close to where he had picked up his victims, leave the boat and head north on foot. Almost as soon as he had stepped ashore, he found himself confronted by the lean figure of a soldier.

"Howdy," greeted Kiowa Cotton and slipped his bowie knife from its sheath. "I reckon you and me'd best have us a lil talk."

## CHAPTER FOURTEEN

## Fetch My Gun Box, Block

Although Captain Douglas St. John Staunce had recovered from the blow on the head while being transported to the main house, he had managed to prevent his captors from realizing that he was conscious. At first, the motion of being half dragged and half carried had hidden his involuntary reactions to recovering. Then he had had sufficient presence of mind to understand that resistance would avail him nothing. He was unarmed and in no physical shape to try to fight off two heavier men. So, instead of struggling futilely, he continued to dangle limply in their hands and allowed his strength to ebb back slowly.

On reaching the mansion's front door, Block kicked at it until Oscar came and admitted them. Shoving by the butler, the sergeant and Grilpan hauled their burden across the hall and into the diningroom. Still maintaining his pose of being unconscious, Staunce peered about him through slitted eyes. Coming to their feet at the big table, Major Lyle and Monica Cable—who was dressed elegantly and displayed no alarm at the intrusion—gazed at the newcomers.

"We got him, major," Block announced unnecessarily. "Grilpan had to club him down, but he's still alive."

"Put him on a chair and search him," Lyle ordered. "Was he alone?"

"Nobody's with him," Block answered evasively.

Realizing the futility of opposition at the moment, Staunce allowed the enlisted men to carry out their superior's wishes. Once his fake identification documents had been removed, he began to groan his way convincingly towards "consciousness." Lyle studied the documents, then flung them onto the table. Filling a glass with water, he strolled forward and flung its contents into the Englishman's face. Staunce reacted naturally, for his eyes had been closed and he was not expecting to be doused. Jerking and almost falling off the chair, he shook his head, opened his eyes and glared around.

"What—Where—How—?" Staunce gasped, using the Teutonic accent but slurring the words as if he had just recovered. "What's the meaning of this? Why was I attacked?"

"Why were you sneaking about the island?" Lyle countered and indicated the documents on the table. "If you're Captain *Rudolph* Schmidt—"

"I'm not. My name is *Ludwig* Schmidt," Staunce corrected, knowing that the major was trying to trap him.

"If you *are* Captain *Ludwig* Schmidt, of the Adjutant General's Department, you could have come across the bridge openly and with full military honours."

"Not if what Miss Cable told us—"

"The little bitch did go to Culver's headquarters, Kade!" Monica yelped.

"Keep your yapper closed!" Lyle commanded, scowling at the woman. Then he swung his cold gaze back to the Englishman. "What did Miss Cable tell you, captain?"

"That, going by the way your men treated the coloured folks here, she believed you must be Rebels in disguise," Staunce answered.

"She was a Reb herself," Monica put in.

"And I told you to keep out of this!" Lyle roared, swinging around with a fury that made its recipient cringe back. Once more he turned his attention to Staunce. "And you came here *alone* to find out if her story was true?"

"Who says I'm alone?"

"There was only him and that nigger kid who run off with the gal in the boat," Block interjected, neither knowing nor caring that Oscar was listening in the hall.

"Where's he now?" Lyle wanted to know. "The nigger kid, I mean."

"At the bottom of the lake," Block replied. "I had to kill him and Titus took him out to get rid of him."

Only by exercising all his will power did Oscar prevent himself from letting the occupants of the diningroom know that he had overheard the words. Turning, he walked swiftly and silently to the rear door and passed through it.

"You should have killed Titus while you were at it," Lyle sniffed. "If he talks, we could have trouble with the rest of them."

"We can soon enough settle anything they start," Block grinned.

"That sounds like the talk I'd expect from Rebels," Staunce commented. "Not from an officer and sergeant of the Union Army."

"Come on now, Schmidt," Lyle scoffed. "You're too intelligent to pretend to believe we're fighting this War to let a few black bastards have freedom."

"Titus doesn't know who was with me," Staunce warned, not taking that aspect of the conversation any further. "All he saw was myself and Eric."

"And you've got a large escort close by?" asked Lyle.

"Is it likely I'd come here unescorted?" Staunce replied, exuding calm confidence.

Lyle did not answer immediately. From Titus's arrival with news of the "Yankee" officer wanting to visit the island secretly, the major had sensed an even greater threat to his secret ambitions than had been posed when Conrad Blucher had arrived.

Ever since Lyle had first heard of Cable's machines, he had realized their full potential. Monica—an old friend—had contrived to keep him informed of her husband's activities, even after war had been declared. Having seen an opportunity to lay his hands on something of great value, Lyle had set about obtaining the means to do so. When deciding to expend his fortune on the organization of a small Army unit, he had given considerable thought to what form it would take. Having no wish to be killed in action, he had considered that the Artillery offered him a solution; but only a partial one. When the time came to put his scheme into operation, he wanted a fighting force to back up his play.

Eventually Lyle had reached the compromise. Using his

contacts in New York, he had gathered sufficient men for
two fifty-strong companies. In addition, he had enlisted the
aid of Stabruck—an Artillery officer with social and political ambitions—and a balloonist. The latter would be a
means of drawing much needed attention to the next item
of Lyle's equipment. Although calling his outfit Artillery,
he had only purchased one cannon; the massive Parrot 30-
pounder. For the rest, his men drilled as Cavalry and were
armed with Spencer repeaters. They were, he had insisted,
to become a specialized Artillery group.

By making representations in the appropriate places,
Lyle had arranged for his outfit to be sent to Arkansas.
They were such an unconventional unit that, even though
short of men, General Culver had never found a use for
them. In the excitement of pursuing the Rebels towards the
Ouachita River, Lyle's command had been left behind and
almost forgotten. As far as he knew, nobody in the Army
of Arkansas was aware of his presence at Cable Grange.

A shrewd businessman, Lyle had always realized that
Cable's revolutionary machines would not sell in large
quantities unless the public could be conditioned to accept
them. To gain this acceptance, they would have to prove
their worth in a spectacular manner. So he had worked out
the means to raise them into prominence. Once they had
helped to bring about a Northern victory in Arkansas, he
would find no difficulty in raising sufficient capital to
make more of them. When the War ended, especially if his
machines had helped to bring it about, he would be in a
position to turn out peace-time versions and have civilians
willing to buy them.

That could all be spoiled, however, if any hint of the
machines' capabilities were made public before the completion of the scheme. So, even if "Schmidt" was genuine
—and Lyle did not doubt that he was—he could not be
permitted to leave the island. He must be killed, in an
acceptable manner, before his escort—assuming that he
had one—missed him. Then, when they came to investigate, Lyle would have had time to think up a suitable excuse for his outfit's continued presence on the island.

"Do you know what I think you are?" Lyle inquired, having reached that final conclusion.

"No," Staunce answered, although a memory stirred and started to give him a warning of what might be coming.

"I think you're a Rebel spy and a liar," Lyle said.

"Then I'll call up my men," Staunce replied, starting to rise. "That—"

"I said you're a stinking traitor and a liar," Lyle repeated.

With that, the major lashed the back of his left hand against Staunce's right cheek. Slammed down on the chair's seat, the Englishman responded in a natural manner.

"You bastard!" Staunce shouted furiously and made as if to leap at his assailant.

"What's ailing you, Oscar?" Mama Lukie demanded worriedly, as her husband entered their small, comfortably furnished and spotlessly clean home close behind the main house.

"It's Eric," the butler croaked, sinking into a chair.

*"Eric?"* the big woman repeated. "I've had this feeling all night that something was wrong with that boy. What's happened?"

"He—He was killed by the Yankees!" Oscar answered, tears trickling down his cheeks.

"Where?" Mama Lukie asked. "How?"

"On the island. Titus brought him and a Yankee officer here. That Sergeant Block said he'd killed Eric and Titus was fixing to drop his body into the lake."

"Lordy lord!" the woman ejaculated.

Although visibly shaken by the news, Mama Lukie retained her self control. She too was crying as she poured out a cup of coffee and placed it before her husband. Then she asked him for more details. Having taken a drink, Oscar braced his shoulders and complied. There was not much more that he could tell her, but at the second mention of Titus's part in the affair, she nodded her head.

"He allus was a mean, untrusting feller," the woman said quietly.

"What're we going to do now, Mama Lukie?" Oscar wanted to know. "With Massa Cable and Miss Harry both gone, there's nothing to hold none of us here."

"Nothing 'cept all them fellers, their rifles and that there big cannon that's guarding the boats. The fellers who does guard on the back've been told to use it if we tries to leave. And they wouldn't think twice about doing it, even though there'd be women 'n' children in the boats."

Oscar nodded his agreement. Shortly after their arrival, the Yankees had brought in added means of protecting the island. The "cannon" was one of three Vandenburg volley guns which had been left behind when the Army of Arkansas went after the retreating Rebels.* While two of the guns were placed to sweep the bridge, the third had been situated so that it could cover the landing beach. It was not kept manned, but the sentries in that area all knew how to fire it and its ninety-eight barrels would spew out their loads like a gigantic shotgun.

"What're we going to do?" the butler insisted.

"Nothing rash, that's for sure," Mama Lukie answered. "Do you reckon you can go back there and act natural?"

"I—" Oscar said hesitantly, then stiffened his body. "I reckon I can."

"Then do it," the woman ordered. "It's lucky that it's my night off, they won't miss me. Don't you let on you know what's happened."

"I won't."

"Comes morning, we'll think some more on what to do."

"How about Titus?" Oscar asked bitterly.

"Don't you go fretting none about him," Mama Lukie advised, nodding towards the big, locked chest in the corner of the room. "I allus figured I'd one day have to

* These Vandenburg volley guns were the other half of the battery destroyed by Staunce's howitzers at the Battle of Martin's Mill. Having heard that they had been left behind, while collecting the William's rapid fire cannon, Lyle had appropriated them for his own use.

give him his come-uppance, for scoffing at me being a
conjure woman. Now he's come to where I've got to do it.
You stay away for a while."

"I'll do that sure enough," Oscar promised and left.

Having locked the door and made certain that all the
drapes were closed at the windows, Mama Lukie opened
the box. From it, she took a small bag of some kind of
skin. Going to the table, she sat down and unfastened the
bag's draw string to take something out. It proved to be a
clay figure shaped like a tall, lanky man and with human
hair, black and crinkly, attached to the head.

"Titus," Mama Lukie said in an awful tone, turning the
figure around in her fingers. "You're going to pay for getting my boy killed."

Having positioned themselves for such an eventuality,
suspecting that their officer might try to provoke a duel,
Block and Grilpan grabbed Staunce by the shoulders and
forced him to remain seated. While the Englishman's
cheeks were flushed red with anger, he did not struggle for
long. A realization of what was happening flooded over
him. Like Conrad Blucher, he was being manipulated into
a position from which he could be killed.

Instantly, although no sign of it showed on the outside,
the Englishman became calm. Ceasing his attempts to
throw off the detaining hands of his captors, he glared at
Lyle.

"This's about what I'd expect of a bunch of lousy, cowardly deserters who're hiding here while good men are
killed in the fighting," Staunce stated, in tones of deepest
contempt.

An ugly red flush crept across Lyle's face at the scath-
ing words, for he knew that was how many soldiers would
regard his actions. Instead of him provoking the quarrel,
the tables had been turned. He stood for a moment, quivering with rage. Then, making an obvious effort, he held his
temper in check.

"That's a remark I don't intend to overlook, captain!"
Lyle declared, spitting out each word as if it was burning

his mouth. "In fact, I'm going to demand that you give me satisfaction for it."

"Duelling's illegal, major," Staunce pointed out.

"Are you trying to avoid facing me?" Lyle challenged.

"No," Staunce assured him. "I'll give you your satisfaction. But I'll need a weapon—unless you plan to be the only one of us who is armed."

"I don't!" Lyle growled. "Fetch my gun box, Block."

"Yo!" the sergeant grunted.

"I'll have your Colt before you go," Lyle continued. "Just in case the captain tries to avoid his obligations."

"Sure," Block replied and complied with the order.

"You can go to bed, Monica," the major commanded— and there was no other way of describing the manner with which he addressed the woman—accepting the non-com's Army Colt.

For once, Monica did not argue. She remembered that she had never found Lyle so passionate as on the night after he had killed Blucher. Deciding that a similar incident would bring identical, or perhaps even better, results, she advanced to kiss the major lightly on the cheek. Then she followed Block from the room. At no time had she shown the slightest pity, or interest, for the captive.

"So we're using *your* weapons, huh?" Staunce said.

"The choice is mine, as the affronted party," Lyle pointed out. "They're a matched pair of revolvers and you'll have first pick at them."

"And if I refuse?" Staunce challenged.

"I'll have you shot as a spy," Lyle informed him. "To-night. Don't think your uniform will save you. My men are well-paid, loyal and obedient."

"And what happens if I win?"

"With me dead, I doubt if my men would stop you leaving."

There was something in the major's answer, Staunce concluded. In the event of him killing Lyle, the enlisted men might decide on discretion being the better part of valour. Having seen Staunce accepted by the major as an officer in the Union Army, they could decide that it would be unsafe to continue with the affair.

In the final analysis, Staunce knew that he must take his chance. He preferred to fight for his life and hoped that he might win.

Sergeant Block entered, carrying the gun box.

In Mama Lukie's house, the lamp had been turned down low. Holding the little clay figure between her fingers, she sat rigid in her chair. Her face was wet with perspiration and a toneless chant came from her lips. Oblivious of everything, even the sound of the shot which came from the main house, she took the head of the figure between the thumb and forefinger of her left hand, holding the body enfolded in her right. Tensing as if preparing to make a great effort, she let out an eerie, frightening grunt and twisted at the tiny head. Then she sat rigid, staring blindly ahead.

Having heard Titus' story—the truth, for the man was too terrified to lie—Kiowa sheathed the bowie knife.

"What you going to do with me, mister?" Titus inquired worriedly.

"Take you back to Cap'n Fog," the Texan answered. "Get Eric's horse and don't try anything."

Approaching the horse, Titus prepared to mount. He had gripped the horn and was placing his left foot into the stirrup iron when the horse, for no apparent reason, reared. Taken by surprise, Titus was pitched away from the animal. Kiowa swept his revolver from its holster, swinging around to try to discover what had startled the horse. Failing to find out, he approached the motionless figure that was sprawled on the ground.

"Get up!" Kiowa ordered.

When Titus did not obey, the Texan knelt by him. Taking out and lighting a match, Kiowa looked down. Holstering his gun, he used his fingers to check on the evidence of his eyes.

"Well I'm damned!" Kiowa breathed, standing up. "I've seen many a man pitched by a hoss and even a couple's'd bust their necks. But I never saw one who bust his neck so bad without even landing on it."

\* \* \*

In general, the setting up of the duel went as it had with Conrad Blucher. Staunce was allowed to examine the weapons, without touching them, and satisfied himself that they were both fully loaded. He then selected the Tranter Army revolver that he wished to use and Block set it down on the table.

When starting the count, Block noticed that Lyle's hand was held at the same height as "Schmidt's," about eight inches over the weapon's butt, instead of being higher. Clearly the major regarded this latest interloper as being far more dangerous than the previous one.

For his part, Lyle was fully aware of the danger. This was no civilian, but a tough, efficient, trained soldier. However, the major felt confident in the advantages given to him by his imported weapons. Watching "Schmidt," in the hope of discovering traces of alarm, Lyle became uneasy. Unless he missed his guess, the captain was not over impressed by his air of mocking self-satisfaction. Certainly it was having far less observable effect than it had had against the Southron newspaper owner.

Alert for treachery, yet not willing to make a move before the count reached its assigned number, Staunce studied his enemy. That Lyle felt confident of success was certain, despite everything seeming to be fair and above board. The Englishman could not shake off a nagging feeling that there must be a joker somewhere in the deck.

"Four!" Block said.

Without waiting for the count to go further, Lyle's hand started to drop.

"Five!" the Yankee sergeant said quickly.

Having already seen the danger, Staunce dipped his right palm on to the handle of the waiting Tranter. Swiftly as he moved, he was just that vital shade too slow. Lyle was already starting to lift his weapon.

From the first moment that the Englishman's fingers began to hook under and close around the Tranter's butt, he started to realize where his enemy's ace-in-the-hole lay. Staunce had fired a Tranter a couple of times, but that had been before he came to fight for the Confederate States. Since then, he had used an 1860 Army Colt, which was a very different proposition.

The Tranter's handle did not offer the smooth, hand-fitting curve of the Colt and could not be grasped so readily. For all that, Staunce managed to commence raising his weapon.

But not as swiftly as Lyle's Tranter was lifting into alignment!

There was another, even more radical difference between the Army Colt and the Tranter. One which was to cost Staunce dearly.

While the Englishman was aware that the Tranter operated by a double-action mechanism, that fact failed to register in his mind under the stress of the situation. Instead, his thumb automatically—and without the need for conscious thought—tried to draw the hammer to full cock, as would have been necessary if he was using a single-action Colt. When the thumb did not locate the hammer's spur that he was seeking, he became confused and flustered.

And that at a time when every split second was of vital importance.

Smoothly adopting his double-handled hold, Lyle took rapid and careful aim. While raising the Tranter, he had also started to squeeze the trigger. He had no need to make himself recollect that the weapon's hammer did not carry a spur by which it could be thumb-cocked. The mechanism had caused the hammer to have almost reached its rearmost position by the time the barrel was pointing in the Englishman's direction. Continuing to manipulate the trigger, the major allowed the hammer to be propelled forward once more.

With his borrowed revolver still a long way from a position in which he could use it to protect himself, Staunce knew that he was beaten.

Flame gushed from the muzzle of Lyle's Tranter and its bullet flew true. He had aimed for an instant kill and achieved his desire. Struck in the head, Staunce discarded the second Tranter. He was twisted away from the table and measured his length upon the floor.

As against Blucher and Lyle's previous pair of victims, training and experience had proved to be the deciding factor.

"You'd better make sure that the back of the island's guarded extra carefully tonight, Block," Lyle ordered, lowering his smoking revolver. "And I want a couple of men out there every night from now on. You'll personally make sure that they keep a damned sight better watch than they have been doing. He's the second bastard to have landed."

"Sure," Block answered sullenly, not caring for the extra work carrying out the order would entail. "What about when his escort comes looking for him?"

"We'll just say that he never arrived," Lyle answered. "And I'll count on you to help me see that nobody says different."

While Staunce had died, he had also prevented his captors and killer from suspecting his true identity and purpose on the island.

## CHAPTER FIFTEEN

# I've Never Had a Coloured Gal

"Captain Dustine Edward Marsden Fog!" Harriet Cable said, her quietly spoken words redolent of deepest suspicion, as she continued to manipulate the pair of oars with some ability. "Are you *sure* that you don't know how to row a boat?"

"Like I told you, we don't need boats down home to Rio Hondo County," the small Texan replied evasively, but in no louder tones than the girl had used. "And seeing's how you-all've showed that you can do it so quietly and well, I'm happy to sit back here and let you go on doing it."

"Why thank you, 'most to death," the girl sniffed, using an expression which she had heard her companion employ on occasion. "You're a Southron gentleman for sure."

"I'm not supposed to be a *Southron* gentleman right now," Dusty pointed out and looked down at his blackened hands. "Anyway, it's all your own fault that you're doing the rowing."

"How do you mean?"

"It was you who pointed out that the Yankees might be keeping a better guard on the back of the island, seeing that Mr. Blucher and Doug had managed to land. And how those Yankees would likely expect to see a coloured *girl* doing the rowing when she and her beau came to call."

"There's times when I talk so much that it hurts," Harry declared ruefully, although she knew that her presence at the oars might go a long way towards convincing any watchers that she and the small Texan were a couple of young Negroes casually visiting the island. "I don't suppose we could go back and fetch those two Yankee prisoners to do the rowing?"

"That'd be against the conventions of war," Dusty pointed out.

"Somebody should make conventions for protecting poor innocent girls like me from men like you," Harry groaned, then became serious. "What do you think has happened to Doug, Dusty?"

"I don't know," the small Texan answered and all the levity—which, to be fair to her, Harry had used as a means of reducing her understandable nervous tension—came to an end. He knew that he could rely upon her not to panic if the situation should turn the wrong way. "But I hope I can find out before we come away."

It was close to eleven o'clock on the night following Captain Douglas St. John Staunce's capture; which was all his companions knew for certain regarding his fate. The girl and Dusty were on their way to Cable's island to make contact with the Negroes, as the Englishman apparently had been unable to do so. A secondary part of their mission was to try to find out what had happened to Staunce and, if he should still be alive and the chance presented itself, to try to rescue him.

Having given Titus's body the same kind of treatment that Eric's had received, Kiowa had hidden the boat. Then he had ridden the three horses in a relay to make the best possible speed and rejoin Company "C" without delay. On his arrival, he had found that his companions had picked up two enlisted men from Captain Stabruck's scattered command. Being city dwellers, they and the others who had fled the scene of the ambush had soon found themselves in difficulties when separated from their experienced leaders. Only chance had brought the pair in the correct direction. Gathered in by Dusty's flank riders, they had been only too pleased to surrender if doing so caused them to be fed. Hoping that he could make use of the pair later, Dusty had been only too willing to feed them and accept the slight extra work involved in guarding them.

Calling together Harry, her father, the two sergeant majors and sergeants, Dusty had had them listen to Kiowa's report. The scout had told them all he had learned from Titus and mentioned the strange manner in which the traitor had died, but without attempting to offer any explanation for the circumstances. Possibly only Cable and Harry, due to their long association with Negroes, came close to guessing the truth. The engineer had mentioned his theory of how Titus' neck had come to be broken, but that aspect had not received any debate. Far more important at that moment had been that if—impossible as it might have seemed—Mama Lukie was involved in her nephew's death, she must have known that her son had been murdered by the Yankees and much more.

"In which case," Cable had stated, "she'll be all the more willing to help us get the rest of her people away from the island."

Although Dusty had hoped that his English *amigo* might be held as a prisoner, he was secretly resigned to the thought that Staunce was probably dead. Maybe even killed in a similar duel to the one which had ended Conrad Blucher's life.

Dusty had refused to let concern for Staunce's welfare distract him from his duty. So he had stated his intentions. There had been strong protests from Sergeant Majors Billy Jack and Smalley when Dusty had said that he personally would visit the island. Neither man's arguments had come close to swaying the small Texan from his resolve.

As always, Dusty was not charging blindly or emotionally into a desperately perilous situation. He had known something of the risks involved and had set about finding a means of circumventing, or reducing, them. So he had asked for and listened to his companion's suggestions. One thing had been obvious from the beginning. It was hardly a task that could be carried out by a single man. So they had started to decide who should go with Dusty. Having allowed the men to say their pieces, Harry had dropped her bombshell. Quietly, without fuss, she had declared her intention of accompanying the small Texan.

No amount of argument, nor grim warnings of the great danger involved, on Dusty's or Cable's part had served to dissuade Harry. In fact, despite all his misgivings, the young captain had been compelled to admit that the arguments she was putting up made good sense.

Harry knew the area, both Nimrod Lake and the island, like the back of her hand. Even more important, Mama Lukie knew and trusted her. It would never do for Cable to be recaptured by Lyle. Neither of his Negro assistants could be spared from their work in helping to keep Pulling Sue and the big gun moving, even if they had had the kind of reckless disregard for danger that was necessary for such a hazardous undertaking.

Having considered all the girl's points, the men had been forced to concede that—apart from the very great element of danger involved—she was the best choice for Dusty's companion.

Even Cable had grudgingly gone along with the majority. After which, they had set about considering how best Dusty and the girl could go about the visit. The Cables' local knowledge proved invaluable in this matter. The engineer had told Dusty of a friend who lived in the vicinity and who could be trusted to render every assistance.

After formulating a line of action for the girl and himself, Dusty had given orders to his men. There was no cover for over a mile on the northern side of the lake; but Billy Jack was to take half of Company "C" as near as he could without being detected by the guards on the bridge. If they should hear shooting—not a single shot, Dusty had insisted, but sufficient firing to know that the Negroes were being attacked—they were to charge down and attempt to effect a rescue. If they were fortunate, the Yankees would be so occupied with the Negroes that the Texans could arrive before the Vandenburg Volley Guns were turned upon them.

The remainder of Company "C" was to remain south of the Fourche la Fave River, under Sergeant Major Smalley's command. In the event of Dusty's and Harry's attempt and the other Texans' rescue bid failing, the Englishman was to destroy Pulling Sue and the Big Gun. Then he was to allow Cable to decide on his own future, but must return with his howitzers to the Confederate States' side of the Ouachita River.

Visiting her family's friends, Harry and Dusty had obtained the items they required to disguise themselves. The girl was wearing a sun bonnet, old blouse and a too-large skirt over her shirt, breeches and riding boots. For his part, Dusty had exchanged his Jeff Davis hat, tunic and gunbelt for a battered straw hat, patched shirt and ancient trousers. He retained his breeches and Hessian boots, hoping—as Harry did regarding her male attire—that the borrowed garments would conceal them for as long as was necessary.

While their outer clothing and having all visible skin blackened by soot would not have stood up to even a casual inspection by daylight, they hoped that it would be sufficient at night to lull the sentries into a sense of false security. That could be very, *very,* important.

Knowing that the fourteen inches' length and not inconsiderable bulk of the Colt 1860 Army revolver did not render it an easily concealed weapon, Dusty had concluded that he could not carry even one of them on his person. Instead, the weapon belt, with its matched revolvers, was wrapped in a burlap sack under the rear seat. Harry, who was less likely to be searched, carried her Colt Pocket Pistol thrust into the rear of her breeches' waistband. Extracting it quickly in an emergency would be impossible, but she had been warned by her companion that she must attempt to use it only as a last resort.

At sundown, Dusty and Harry had been guided by Kiowa to the hidden boat. Billy Jack was already making a long circle to place his detail into their supporting position. On the southern side of the lake, Cable and Smalley had already selected the area from which—if all went well— they would use the big gun the following morning.

On boarding the little boat and concealing his weapons, Dusty had been ready to do the rowing. Harry had stated that to do so might strike any guards who saw them as being out of character. Although the majority of Negro men did not loaf around while their women did all the work, the type of soldiers enlisted by Lyle believed that they did. So any watcher would be less likely to suspect the couple's arrival, even after dark, if Dusty was acting in what would most likely be regarded as in keeping with a coloured man's normal, shiftless behaviour.

Leaving Kiowa to take care of their horses, Harry had

started to row the boat across the lake and towards the rear side of the island. At the conclusion of the brief, quietly spoken conversation, she looked at the *big* young Texan. Thinking of what lay ahead, she found herself taking comfort from remembering the stories of his prowess and capabilities which various members of Company "C" had told to her during the journey north. Sensing that there had been much truth in the tales, she considered Dusty ought to have a better than fair chance of pulling them through the perils of the visit.

While talking, Dusty was also examining his destination. Like Nimrod Lake, the island was roughly oblong in shape and extended from east to west. Although the Cables had assured him that the landing beach could not be seen from the guards' quarters by the bridge, there was little cover available on any side.

As Dusty had expected, the two cressets were glowing on the main landing area of the shore. After two visitations, Lyle could be counted upon to strengthen the efficiency of his guards and their aids. None of the soldiers were in evidence, which did not rule out the possibility that one or more could be watching from the darkness. That was why he had asked Harry to make for the boats which had been drawn up under the lights and above the water's level. To have gone elsewhere would have been certain to arouse suspicion.

At first Dusty was puzzled by why Lyle, making use of Cable's Negro employees, had not placed more cressets along the bank. Then the answer had become obvious. Just beyond the eastern fringe of the light, he could make out the massive bulk of the third Vandenburg Volley gun and, close by, a shelter built to protect the ammunition supply on the caisson. The gun was positioned to sweep the beach, making an unauthorized departure very hazardous.

"What's wrong?" Harry inquired as she saw Dusty stiffen slightly.

"There's at least one of them waiting for us!" the small Texan replied. "I saw just a little glint of something metallic over by the caisson."

"Just one man?"

"That's all I could see."

"What shall we do?"

"Keep on going in," Dusty ordered. "If we swerve away, he'll maybe challenge, or even throw lead at us. Either way, we'd never get in again tonight."

"Do you want me to go into the light?" Harry wanted to know.

"Can you make it look like you're trying to, but're being pulled by?"

"It shouldn't be hard."

"Go towards the Vandenburg," Dusty requested.

*"Towards* it?" the girl breathed.

"Why sure," Dusty confirmed. "That way, the feller'll think we haven't seen him and don't have any bad notions. It'll put him even more off his guard."

"You could be right," Harry admitted, but contrived to sound as if she doubted he would be.

Watching the manner in which the girl was handling the boat, Dusty silently conceded that he could not have done it so well. She was bringing to bear all the experience she had gained during her tomboy childhood. In those days, she had spent many hours rowing on the lake. They were not sufficiently far behind for her to have lost her touch. With swiftly taken glances over her right shoulder, she kept the bows pointing towards the dark bulk of the Volley Gun.

"Land-sakes, Mandy!" Dusty said in a loud voice and with a pretty fair impersonation of an exasperated Negro's voice. "Why'n't you-all head for the lights?"

"I'm trying, Jethro, I'm trying!" Harry answered, sounding even more realistic. "If you-all wasn't such a shiftless no-account, it'd be you rowing this boat, not me."

"It ain't fitten for a gentleman with his freedom to row," Dusty explained, using an excuse which he felt sure would be accepted by the listening soldier. "That's woman's work."

Even as the words were leaving Dusty's lips, he became aware that there was not one, but *two* soldiers. The second had been standing against the gun and had been unnoticed until his companion joined him.

"You keep abusing me!" Harry shrilled. "And it won't be no *love*-potion I gets from Mama Lukie."

Keeping up a torrent of protests, the girl guided the boat into the shallows until the bows grounded. Complaining bitterly at her "stupidty" in having landed them away from the lights, Dusty rose and stepped over the side. He left his weapons aboard, for he was not counting on them as a means of quelling the sentries. On Harry joining him, they waded ashore. They did not enter the illuminated section, yet avoided conveying the impression that they were deliberately staying away from it.

"Hold it right there!" barked a harsh voice from one of the dark shapes which Dusty was overtly watching.

"Yipes!" the small Texan yelped, while Harry acted equally alarmed, "Who-all's there?"

Advancing, the pair of large figures proved to be a sergeant, with empty hands—but whose weapon belt carried a holstered revolver and a sabre—and an enlisted man armed with a Spencer rifle. Footsteps sounded at the far side of the lighted area and a second burly, rifle-toting soldier hurried across it.

"Who're you pair," Sergeant Block demanded, "and what're you doing here?"

"We've come to see Mama Lukie, sir," Dusty answered, studying the trio as they converged upon him and the girl.

"At this time of the night?" Block growled.

"It's all Mandy's fault, sir," Dusty explained humbly. "She just wouldn't row no faster."

"'Tain't my place to row—!" Harry began indignantly.

"Where've you pair come from?" Block interrupted.

"The French place, sir," Dusty supplied, using the name of a family along the Fourche la Fave River who were suspected of having Union sympathies. "We'd've been here sooner only Mandy wouldn't row—"

"Don't you-all keep on about my rowing, Jethro!" Harry shrilled.

"She's not bad looking, or shaped, Blocky," Grilpan remarked. "I've never had a coloured gal, have you?"

"Nope," the sergeant admitted and his right hand passed to draw the sabre from its sheath. With the weapon dangling at his side, he moved to his left. "I don't see why Lyle should be the only one to have him a mite of woman-fun. Anything else on the lake, Dasour?"

"Not's I can see," the second enlisted man answered, slowing his pace and looking across the water.

All the time the conversation had been taking place, Dusty was keeping the soldiers under observation. After Block had drawn the sabre, Grilpan leaned his Spencer against the Vandenburg. Dasour was still several yards away, strolling along leisurely with his rifle at the trail.

Although Harry realized what the soldiers' comments were implying, she displayed no hint of her knowledge. Instead, she continued to berate Dusty for his insults to her rowing ability. At the same time, she edged towards the water. That gave Dusty an excuse to turn his back on the soldiers. Just as he had hoped, Grilpan came up behind him. In all probability, the soldier intended to attack him from the rear.

Suddenly, without giving a warning of his intentions, Dusty took a step in Grilpan's direction. The soldier spread apart his arms, ready to engulf his victim. Back hurled the small Texan's right arm bending as it moved. The point of his elbow smashed, with all the power of his muscular young body behind it, full into the Yankee's *solar plexus*. It was a devastating blow, delivered with force and precision. Completely unprepared, Grilpan felt as if he had been struck in the chest by a cannonball. Letting out a strangled, agonized croak, he blundered to the rear.

As soon as Dusty had completed the attack on Grilpan, he turned his attention to the sergeant. An experienced brawler, Block had had his suspicions lulled by the visitor's appearances and behaviour. So he had not expected such violent opposition on the part of what he assumed to be a small, insignificant Negro. He very quickly learned that appearances could be deceptive. Unfortunately, the lesson was not one from which he would derive any lasting benefit.

Pivoting to the right as he completed the attack on Grilpan, Dusty drew his bent left arm across his chest. Then he reversed his direction and used the momentum of his turn

to provide impetus as his arm extended and swung in an
arc. He held his left hand clenched, but did not strike in the
conventional Occidental manner. Instead, he used it as the
*uraken*, back fist, of *karate* as he had been taught by his
uncle's Japanese servant.

The protruding root of Dusty's second finger struck
Block just under the nose, grinding savagely into the phil-
trum collection of nerves in the centre of the top lip. Raw
agony ripped through the sergeant, blinding him with involuntary tears and causing him to release his grasp of the
sabre as he reeled back a few steps. The point of the
weapon spiked into the ground and it stood almost erect.

Still moving with the same devastating speed, Dusty
rushed towards Dasour. Swerving around the nearest of the
boats, the man skidded to a halt. For a vitally important
moment, he was frozen into immobility by what he was
seeing happen to his companions. Belatedly, he tried to
bring his rifle into a firing position.

Sprinting forward, Dusty sprang into the air. As he rose,
he drew up and bent his right leg. At the height of his leap,
he thrust forward the leg. The bottom of his foot smashed
as hard as his gluteus muscles could force it against the top
of Dasour's chest. As Dusty rebounded from the leaping
side kick, the soldier was pitched backwards. Dasour's legs
struck the side of the boat and he overbalanced. Falling
backwards, his shoulders crashed into the opposite side and
his head snapped downwards with an audible crack.

"Dusty!" Harry cried, reaching behind her and trying to
liberate the Pocket Pistol as she stared from Block to Grilpan.

The latter was hanging against the side of the Vandenburg, trying to refill his lungs. Already, however, the sergeant was wiping his eyes with his left knuckles, while his
right hand clawed at the flap of his holster.

Alighting from the kick, Dusty flung himself back in the
way from which he had come. Reaching out, he caught
hold of the sabre and plucked it from the ground. Instantly,
he realized that it was not the heavy, awkward, U.S. Army
Model of 1840 pattern that was unflatteringly known as the
"Old Wrist-Breaker." In size, weight and balance, it came

close to his own Haiman Brothers' sabre. Looking down, he realized that he held Staunce's British-made Light Artillery weapon. That implied that his friend was dead. Probably the sergeant was responsible for whatever had happened to Staunce and had also killed Eric.

Already Block had the holster flap open and the Colt was coming from it. Two bounding strides carried Dusty into range and he delivered a back hand swing. Although Block saw what was coming, his brain reacted far too slowly. Hissing through the air, the edge of the blade sliced into the side of his neck and almost decapitated him. Dusty had no trouble in liberating his weapon.

Harry let out a muffled scream and turned around to hide the hideous sight from her gaze. With the head tilted at an unnatural angle and blood spurting from the wound, Block's body stood for a moment. Then it toppled sideways.

Ignoring the girl for the moment, the small Texan turned on Grilpan. The soldier was clawing at his rifle. Darting forward as if making a *fleche* attack, Dusty lunged and thrust with the sabre. Its point passed below Grilpan's arm and into his chest. Stiffening, Grilpan dropped the rifle. As Dusty withdrew the sabre's blade, he crumpled face down and lay still.

"All right, Harry," Dusty said gently, walking towards the girl. "It's all over now."

"Oh lord!" moaned Harry, feeling as if she would collapse and fetch up. "It was terrible."

"It always is," Dusty answered, taking her by the arm. "Come on. You'd best go and see if you can get to Mama Lukie. While you're doing it, I'll tend to the gun."

Leading Harry behind the Vandenburg, Dusty saved her from needing to look again at the bodies. Then, after watching her hurrying towards the Negroes' homes, he collected his weapons from their boat. Strapping on the gunbelt, he went to the boat in which Dasour was lying. A quick examination told the small Texan that the man was of no further danger to him. In falling backwards, Dasour had broken his neck.

Returning to the Vandenburg, Dusty grasped the handles

of the breech mechanism. Turning them, he unscrewed and drew the breech along its key-way until it tilted upright on the piece's stock. Listening for any sounds to suggest that Harry had been discovered by the Yankees, he removed the ninety-eight cartridges from their individual chambers and tossed each one into the water. After taking out and disposing of the central charge which, on being ignited by a percussion cap, would have set off every cartridge, he closed and screwed home the breech. Reloading the weapon was a lengthy process. So, providing that the Negroes could take to the boats without being detected, they were safe from the Volley Gun.

## CHAPTER SIXTEEN

## We Don't Aim to Get Killed

"I'll hit the island with every shell," Sergeant Major Smalley told Eli Cable as they stood watching the big gun being loaded. "But at this range I couldn't say where in a hundred yards' square the shells'll drop. One thing I'll promise is that I'll try to keep them away from your home."

"I'd rather you tried to avoid hitting my people's homes," the engineer answered. "They'll need somewhere to live and I've an idea that it will be a long time before Harry and I can call Cable Grange our home again."

The evacuation of the island had taken place successfully. On reaching Mama Lukie's house, Harriet Cable had found the old woman ready. It almost seemed that Mama Lukie had used her strange powers and discovered that the attempt would be made. Swiftly the Negress and her husband had alerted the rest of Cable's employees. Although there were guards at the bridge, the rest of the soldiers had been in bed. So the Negroes had been able to slip away undetected. A couple of the boats had been crowded, but there had been sufficient to transport all the party to the southern side of Nimrod Lake in one trip. Dusty's precautions with the Vandenburg had proven to be unnecessary, which did not cause him to regret having taken them.

Having completed the first and most important part of his assignment—Oscar had told him what had happened to Captain Staunce, having witnessed the duel from the garden once more—Dusty had wondered if he could take advantage of the island's unguarded state. Unfortunately, before he could make the necessary arrangements, the alarm had been raised.

What had happened was that, when Sergeant Block did

not return to the guard-house, its occupants became suspicious. Block had never been noted for his devotion to duty and, as there had been an undercurrent of unrest amongst the Negroes all day, the corporal sent soldiers to investigate. They discovered that the houses were deserted and, going to the rear of the island, had found the three bodies. So they had aroused the rest of their party.

Rather than chance losing men, Dusty had decided to wait until dawn and continue with his original idea.

So Dusty was on the northern side of the lake, with half of his Company and the two prisoners. As yet, they had not shown themselves. While they remained in concealment, about a mile from the bridge, he lay hidden behind a bush and kept watch through his field glasses.

Established on a piece of level ground about three thousand, one hundred yards from the island, the Parrot 30-Pounder rifle was being crewed by eight of the mountain battery's most experienced men. All had served with siege guns in the British Army and Smalley felt sure that they could handle their newly acquired piece in a satisfactory manner.

Fixed rounds were not practical for use in such a massive gun, so the load was split into its two major components. Already the three and three-quarters of a pound powder charge had been thrust down the barrel. The twenty-seven and a half pound shell had also been forced home with the cup-headed rifle rammer, which had to be used to prevent pressure igniting the fuse in the shell's nose. With that done, the temporary chief of piece had caused the trail to be levered into alignment and laid the adjustable rear sight upon the workshop. Twirling the elevating screw, he had tilted the barrel to an angle of eight degrees. When all the preparations had been carried out, he grasped the end of the lanyard and retreated to the left and rear of the gun.

"Ready!" the sergeant announced to Smalley.

Before replying, the sergeant major swung his eyes to Harry and Cable. The engineer exchanged glances with his daughter. Setting his face into a grim mask, Cable slowly nodded his head.

"Fire!" Smalley commanded and raised his field glasses to observe the fall of the shell.

Giving a sharp tug at the lanyard, the chief of piece activated the firing process. Causing a deep roar and a gushing cloud of white smoke, the Parrot ejected its shell and bounded rearwards with the force of the recoil. There was no need to hurry with the reloading, for they were not to fire again until a minute had gone by. So the crew turned their gazes to the distant island, as did Harry, her father, and every other man present. Eleven and a half seconds dragged by without anything happening. Just as Harry was thinking that the shell must have missed, or failed to go off, there was an eruption of earth about ten yards to the east of the workshop.

"Did you see the fall, sergeant?" Smalley inquired.

"Yes, sir," answered the non-com.

"Reload and make ready," Smalley ordered. "See if you can get the next one on the target."

In the diningroom of the mansion, Monica Cable was seated at the table and complaining bitterly over the poor service now that the servants had taken their departure. Her words were directed at an entirely unsympathetic Major Lyle. For his part, the officer had other, more serious reasons for being alarmed by the incidents of the previous night. He suspected that the Negroes had learned of "Schmidt's" visit and its consequences. They had been restless ever since Harriet Cable had fled, but it was too much of a coincidence to believe that they would have chosen that particular night to escape. So he was worried about the story they would tell, if they should meet the captain's escort. With Block and Grilpan dead, Lyle might find great difficulty in explaining how "Schmidt" had come to be killed. Nor did the major have such a strong hold over the remainder of his men. It was fears for their own safety, in case the Negroes should return to avenge the insults and humiliations received at the soldiers' hands, rather than a desire to accept discipline which had kept them at their posts and awake all night.

"Don't you have a better cook?" Monica was saying, when the shell arrived and exploded.

Throwing over his chair as he sprang up, Lyle ignored the woman's startled shriek. He darted from the room, across the hall and out of the building. Staring around, he saw a number of his men rushing towards the western end of the island. Sprinting in that direction, he joined them around a smoking crater.

"What happened?" Lyle barked, addressing the corporal who was present.

"I'm damned if I know, major," the non-com replied. "I was down at the guard house and heard the bang."

"It come from over there," one of the enlisted men stated, pointing to the southern side of the lake. "I heard it whistle over, just like when we was training with that big gun."

"The big gun!" Lyle repeated and stared to the south. There was nothing to be seen, but he knew the range of the weapon in question. "Send somebody to fetch my field glasses, corporal!"

Before the order could be carried out, a soldier rushed up. He had come from the bridge and was in a state of wild excitement.

"Riders!" the man yelled. "There's a bunch of 'em coming!"

"What kind of riders?" Lyle demanded.

"Soldiers of some kind," the enlisted man replied. "They're too far off for us to know more than that."

"Come on!" Lyle barked at the corporal.

Followed by his men, in an untidy rabble rather than as a disciplined outfit, the major ran to the bridge. Looking across the water, he studied the approaching party. They were still too far away for details of their clothing to be detectable.

"Who are they?" asked one of the soldiers.

"Rebels," Lyle stated, knowing that the answer would bring about the kind of response that he required. "They may be dressed in our uniforms, so don't trust them."

Even as the major spoke, another shell plunged down. It exploded nearer to the workshop and caused some consternation among the soldiers.

"They're Rebs for sure!" the corporal growled. "You're not armed, major."

"Get the men into position and be ready to fight," Lyle

barked, accepting the comment. "I'll fetch my weapons and join you. If they attack, open fire no matter how they're dressed."

Hurrying towards the house, Lyle was deeply perturbed by the turn of events. Perhaps Harriet Cable's story had been accepted and the Union Army believed that a force of Rebels were holding the island. It seemed highly unlikely that Confederate States' soldiers would be so deep in Union-held territory, especially with a weapon capable of throwing a projectile large enough to make such a crater.

If it came to a point, Lyle doubted if there was any Artillery piece—other than his Parrot—large enough to do it in Arkansas at that time.

Could it be that Stabruck had betrayed him?

Perhaps the captain had been captured by "Schmidt's" escort and, having failed to convince them of his *bona fides*, was compelled to help them take the island.

Lyle believed that Stabruck would do so to save his own skin.

That and other matters churned through Lyle's mind as he approached the main entrance to the mansion. Monica was there, gobbling incoherent questions, but he thrust her aside without answering. Followed by the frightened woman, he entered and made his way upstairs. While he meant to arm himself, he did not intend to rejoin his men until after the shooting had started. In that way, he might be able to confuse the issue when he was called upon to answer for his actions.

Maybe Lyle's men were badly disciplined, but self-preservation had caused them to take up their defensive positions. Sending only a token force to watch the other side of the island, the corporal held the remainder at the bridge. He had collected the field glasses from the guard house and was examining the approaching riders.

"They're Rebs all right!" the corporal announced, then stared harder. "But they've got two of our men. Least, two of 'em's wearing our uniforms."

By that time, the riders had covered about half a mile. They halted, still beyond accurate shooting range, sitting their horses in a line. Through his field glasses the corporal saw the small Rebel captain address somebody to his right.

"One of 'em's coming!" yelled a soldier.

Turning his field glasses, the corporal watched a man leave the grey-clad rank and gallop forward.

"He's one of us!" warned the non-com. "Hell's fire. It's Willie Grombech from the other Company. Don't shoot, none of you!"

Waving his hat over his head and yelling identical advice, Grombech did not reduce speed as he approached the edge of the lake. He galloped over the bridge and brought his horse to a sliding halt.

"What's up, Willie?" the corporal wanted to know.

"You boys'd best get off the island," the newcomer answered, almost tumbling from his saddle in his eagerness. "Those Rebs have the big gun. It's on the other side of the lake—"

"So that's what's been shelling us!" the corporal interrupted, swinging on his heel to gaze in a southerly direction.

"Yeah!" Grombech confirmed. "And it'll keep on doing it until you surrender 'n' march across the bridge."

"Surrender?" repeated the corporal, ignoring the undisciplined roar of conversation that arose from the listening enlisted men.

"That's what Cap'n Fog, him being their boss, said for me to come and tell you," Grombech answered. "There's a company of Texas Light Cavalry and a Reb mountain howitzer battery to back up the big gun. I'd best go and tell Lyle."

"Where's the rest of your crowd?" a man demanded.

"The Rebs took 'em prisoner, then turned them loose again," Grombech replied. "That's what I was told and I believe 'em. They've treated Gus 'n' me good enough since they catched us."

"They're not shelling us no more," the corporal remarked.

"Happen you've not started across the bridge in ten minutes, they will be," Grombech warned. "Cap'n Fog said for me to make sure you all knew *that*."

Looking around, the corporal saw panic rising among

the other men. Not only had they seen examples of the results of the Parrot's shelling, while Stabruck had been training his crews, but they had been fed on stories of its accuracy and lethal capabilities. So they were fully conversant, or thought they were, with the big gun's potential.

"Come on!" one man shouted. "Let's do like the Rebs want!"

"Sure!" another agreed, discarding his rifle. "That's all we can do."

"Hold it, damn you!" the corporal bellowed, staring about him and finding that more of the men were putting or throwing down their weapons. "We'd best hear what Lyle's got to say about it."

"To hell with Lyle!" yelled one of the men who had already disarmed himself. "We don't aimed to get killed by his damned gun. And that's what staying here'll mean."

Going by the rumble of agreement, the majority of the soldiers felt the same way on the subject. At that moment, the potential threat of the big gun was fully justified; although not in a manner which would have met with Lyle's approval.

Faced by the whole of Company "C," even when backed by the mountain howitzers, the Yankees would have been ready and willing to fight back. The little guns' range did not exceed half a mile, which would have brought the crews within the distance over which the Spencer rifles could make hits. The Parrot was so far beyond the capabilities of their weapons that they felt a complete, helpless impotency that was frightening and unnerving.

That was what Dusty Fog had been counting upon happening, his reason for being so determined to capture and bring the big gun to Nimrod Lake. He had laid his plans carefully and the fortunate capture of the two soldiers had presented him with a safe way of delivering his ultimatum. Before dispatching Grombech, the more intelligent of the pair, the small Texan had given him detailed instructions as to what he must say.

"Hey!" the message-bearer put in, recollecting a point which the *big* blond Texas captain had stressed. "We've got to hand over our officers alive."

"How's that?" growled the corporal.

"It's what Cap'n Fog told me," Grombech stated. "We have to fetch our officers over with us when we surrender."

"Let's go and fetch him, then," suggested one of the listening soldiers.

"Come on," a second continued. "Time's a-wasting."

"Don't forget they want him alive!" Grombech warned.

"We'll see they get him that way," the corporal promised, drawing the revolver from his holster.

Followed by most of the enlisted men, the non-com stalked determinedly towards the mansion. He held his weapon concealed behind his back, knowing Lyle's temper and being sure that the major would be unwilling to yield to their demands.

Watching the soldiers heading in the direction of the house, Lyle stepped back from the bedroom window. He held a pair of field glasses, with which he had been studying the situation. Already he had assessed the developments and had drawn conclusions from what he had seen.

With two exceptions, the riders on the northern shore wore Confederate Cavalry uniforms. Perhaps "Schmidt" had been a Rebel in disguise. That would explain why his Union escort had failed to put in an appearance. It also suggested that his whole story had been a tissue of lies.

Harriet Cable must have gone looking for her father and had fallen in with the Confederate Cavalry in the course of her search. Probably she had alerted them to the danger posed by Cable's machines. They had captured Pulling Sue and the Parrot, probably also preventing Stabruck from killing the engineer. To make matters worse, they obviously had men capable of using the big gun.

Seeing Grombech's arrival over the bridge, Lyle had guessed why he was sent. He would be bringing a demand from the Rebels for the surrender of the island. From all appearances, the soldiers had been all too willing to accept. After listening, some had thrown aside their rifles. Then the majority of them had set off towards the house.

They must, Lyle surmised, be coming to fetch him.

Or would it be Monica?

Remembering Cable's reluctance to put the traction engines to martial use, Lyle also recollected how he had made the engineer obey. Possibly the price Cable had extracted from the Rebel for his assistance had been an assurance that Monica would be delivered safely to him.

Crossing the room, Lyle tossed his field glasses on to the bed. He took his weapon belt and was strapping it on as he went to the door. While descending to the entrance hall, he concluded his plans. Capture seemed inevitable and with it, the ruination of his scheme for aggrandizement. Knowing the kind of men he had under his command, he doubted if he could reason with them now that they had decided to surrender. It would be dangerous to try, going by the expressions he had seen on their faces as they approached the mansion. So he would give Monica to them and tell them to hand her over, while he destroyed some imaginary secret documents. His real reason for wanting to be left alone was something quite different. Nobody else was going to profit from his work. The workshop was mined and he needed only a couple of minutes' grace to set off the fuse, making sure that his brain-child did not fall into the Rebels' hands.

"What's happening, Kade?" Monica inquired querulously, as the major joined her by the front door. "Some of the men are coming."

"I know that," Lyle answered and took hold of the woman's left bicep with his right hand. "We'd better go and see."

"I don't wan—" Monica protested, trying to free herself and hold back.

"Come on, damn you!" Lyle growled.

With that, Lyle started to haul the protesting Monica through the door. She held back as best she could, striving to avoid being taken outside. As always, resistance to his desires caused Lyle's temper to boil up and he increased the pressure he was exerting.

Seeing his men at close quarters, Lyle felt a surge of impotent fury building inside him against the Rebels who were responsible for destroying his scheme. All his expectations regarding the effect of the Parrot had been correct. Used as he had intended—and as it had been turned against him—it would have been close to the ultimate weapon. There was a raw fear on every face that came close to the panic he had envisaged once a bombardment was commenced by the big gun. Yet he knew the men to be tough and brave enough under normal conditions. The fear of being shelled without having any means of replying had wrought the change in them. If he had been able to use the big gun as he had hoped to do, he might easily have brought about the South's defeat—

The soldiers surged forward as their officer appeared, pulling the struggling woman behind him.

"Here, men," Lyle said, trying to swing Monica forward. "Take Mrs. Cable to the Rebs."

"It ain't *her* they wants," the corporal replied. "It's you."

"And you're coming!" shouted a private, advancing with his Spencer lined at waist level. "Like it or not!"

Furious at Monica's refusal to co-operate, Lyle had given a harder heave. He exerted all his strength and was propelling the woman towards his men when the meaning of what was being said struck home. Releasing his hold on Monica's arm, he allowed her to blunder helplessly by him. Starting to spring aside, it was his intention to make a run for the workshop and attend to the fuse before being compelled to surrender.

Unable to halt herself, Monica stumbled on to the barrel of the soldier's rifle. With his nerves already strained to breaking point, he involuntarily completed the pressure of his forefinger on the trigger. Down lashed the big side hammer and the Spencer hurled its .56 calibre bullet into the woman's left breast. The soft lead cone smashed its way through her as she was flung backwards and it narrowly missed Lyle.

Ignoring Monica's fate, Lyle began to run. One of the soldiers, remembering that the Rebels wanted his officer alive, hurled his rifle. It struck Lyle's legs, tripping him and sending him crashing down. Before he could recover, several soldiers leapt upon him and he was dragged bodily towards the bridge.

CHAPTER SEVENTEEN

## This Time It's *My* Rules

Major Kade F. Lyle watched Sergeant Major Billy Jack placing the mahogany gun box on the table and opening its lid. Then he turned his attention to the only other occupant of the room.

The time was shortly before sundown and Cable's island was in the hands of the Confederate States' Army. Or had been, for all but the three men had retired across the bridge and were awaiting the completion of the work which had brought them so deep into Union-held territory.

On the surrender of Lyle's men, Captain Dusty Fog had led his party to take charge of the island. In accordance with their orders, the remainder of Company "C," apart from a couple of scouts out on the flanks, had hurried to join their commanding officer and help prevent the Yankees from causing trouble.

Having recovered from his fall, Lyle had had the humiliating experience of seeing the horses, arms and equipment which he had purchased to have used in his scheme being taken over by the enemy. From the comments he had overheard, the Texans were confident that they could deliver their booty safely to their own lines beyond the Ouachita River.

Instead of caring about his unarmed, defenceless men's possible fate, Lyle had been furious to discover that he had been wrong regarding Cable's feelings for Monica. Going by the engineer's remarks, he had known about his wife's infidelity. Lyle had also realized that he was wrong on another matter. Apparently Harriet Cable had told her father of the true state of affairs between his wife and their captor. Having found Harry's door locked, Lyle had not sus-

176

pected that she had been at liberty on the night of Blucher's death. So the major had assumed that nothing more than coincidence had prompted her to leave when she did.

Although distressed by Monica's death, Cable had not been grief-stricken. He had arranged for two of his Negro employees—who had joined him after their escape from the island—to prepare a coffin and dig a grave in a grove far from the island. Then he had taken the remainder of his staff's male members to the workshop. There, they had dismantled such of the machinery as Cable had wanted to save. It and many of the tools had been taken to a cave a couple of miles from Nimrod Lake, to be stored and cared for by the Negroes until such a time as Cable could return and resume his work.

With everything completed, Lyle had been brought to the mansion by Billy Jack and had found Dusty Fog waiting. Everybody else had been told to leave the island, for Lyle's explosives were to be used to destroy Big Minnie.

"What's this all about?" Lyle demanded, although he could guess.

"I think you called it a duel at other times," Dusty Fog replied.

"You mean that *you* expect *me* to fight a duel with *you?*" Lyle growled.

"That's just what I mean," Dusty confirmed.

"And if I refuse?"

"Then I'll take you back with me to stand trial for the murder of Conrad Blucher. I've a witness to prove you did it. Mr. Cable's butler was watching from the garden. And, even if we don't get you for that, you'll hang for the people who were killed by your gun at Arkadelphia."

"I don't know what you're talking about!" Lyle stated, so vehemently that Dusty sensed he was telling the truth. After the small Texan had explained, the major spat out, "That bastard! Damn it, Stabruck wasn't supposed to—"

"Do it until after Big Minnie was ready," Dusty finished for Lyle, when the other's words died away. "Then you'd have had the big gun shell women and children, to make our Army cross the Ouachita."

"If that's what Stabruck told you—!" Lyle began.

"He told us nothing," Dusty interrupted. "We saw through your scheme right from the start. It'll never work now. When we leave here, I'll set off the explosives you had set in the workshop and Big Minnie'll be finished."

"You're sure *you'll* be leaving, if we fight?" Lyle challenged.

"If I don't, I've told my sergeant major that you're to be set free and allowed to rejoin your Army," Dusty answered.

A faint sneer came to Lyle's lips at the words, for he doubted that the lanky, mournful-faced sergeant major would obey in the event of the captain losing the duel. However, the major had no intention of refusing the challenge. While the Rebels could not, in all probability, substantiate their charges of murder, the trial would ruin any hopes Lyle might harbour for the future. Word of the duels would reach the North and were certain to arouse undesirable questions about how his first pair of victims had met their ends. What was more, if mention of the traction engines was to leak out, he would not be able to ensure that he controlled the marketing and production of similar machines.

All of Lyle's present problems were the result of that short, insignificant young Rebel's efforts. Lyle had heard enough during the day to realize that Dusty Fog had been the organizing and driving force behind the capture of the Parrot and its use to bring about the surrender of the island's garrison. He had also smashed into the dirt Lyle's carefully hatched scheme to make a fortune. So, no matter what happened to him after it, the major was determined to take his revenge on the small Texan.

"All right," Lyle gritted. "I'll take you on."

"I thought you might," Dusty drawled. "Billy Jack, let the major pick his weapon and show him that it's still loaded and capped. Then go and put it at the end of the table."

"Yo!" answered the sergeant major, but without making any of his usual doleful comments. There was a job of work to be done, one too serious for the levity which always lay behind his assumed pessimism. "Have whichever 'n' you fancy, major. Only don't try to take it out of the box."

"I'll take the one at the top," Lyle stated.

It was a matter of complete indifference to the officer which revolver he had selected. He knew them both equally well and could handle either with complete confidence.

Everything, Lyle told himself, appeared to be going as it had on the previous occasions; except that he was being granted the first pick of the weapons. He was allowed to see that the designated Tranter had not been tampered with and followed Billy Jack to the end of the table.

For all Lyle's confidence, a nagging train of thoughts started to bite at him.

Why was the small Texan, who had apparently been told about the duels with Blucher and "Schmidt," allowing the affair to be conducted in a similar manner?

Could it be that he was rashly trying to impress the men under his command with his courage, gun-skill and how he was a better *man* than "Schmidt"?

A short, insignificant youngster might easily adopt such tactics without thinking of the consequences. If he should win, he would rise in his men's esteem. Or so the small Texan might imagine would happen.

And yet, Lyle remembered, the hard-bitten veterans of his captor's Company had moved smartly enough when the small Texan had given them orders. There had been no derision, indiscipline, or lack of respect in their attitudes. Rather they had treated the captain with a deference which Lyle had never managed to extract from the men under his command.

Obviously there was more, *much* more, to Captain Fog than met the eye.

So why was he taking an apparently reckless chance?

Turning at the end of the table, Lyle found that Dusty had not moved. Instead of taking the second Tranter to the other end, he remained where he had been all through the conversation. Only about ten feet separated him from Lyle, not the twenty-five feet over which the previous duels had been fought. What was more, the gun box's lid had been closed and the small Texan stood with empty hands thumb-hooked into his Western-style *buscadero* belt.

"Why haven't you taken the other Tranter?" Lyle inquired.

"You use your weapon," Dusty answered. "And I'll use mine."

"Very well," Lyle assented, but could not hold down a twinge of uneasiness as he realized that he had lost one of his greatest advantages. "If you'll go and take your place—"

"This time it's *my* rules, major," Dusty interrupted. "I'll stand *here*. My sergeant major will count to five, then we start shooting."

"Put your revolver on the table—" Lyle commenced.

"Like I said, major," Dusty answered quietly. "It's *my* rules. I'll draw on five, or before if you make a move."

"I don't need that kind of advantage!" Lyle snorted, watching Dusty's hands lift from the belt and point, with fingers slightly hooked and thumbs extended, inwards at the white handles of the Army Colts.

"Major," Dusty replied. "This way, *you* don't have any advantage. Start the count, sergeant major."

"They're your rules," Lyle declared and hoped that he sounded more confident than he now felt. He raised his right hand about eight inches above the Tranter's butt. "I'm ready and on your own head be it."

"One!" Billy Jack commenced.

Despite having had numerous examples of Dusty's capabilities, the lanky sergeant major wondered if he might not be biting off more than he could chew. Billy Jack knew just how fast his young officer could draw and shoot, but he was facing a man who had already killed at least twice in duels. The second time had been when matched with a skilled fighting man. Captain Staunce had been all of that, yet he had fallen before Lyle's revolver in similar circumstances.

"Two!" the sergeant major continued and saw Lyle's right hand quiver as if it was on the point of being set into motion.

At that moment, Lyle was contemplating making a grab

for the Tranter. Even as the notion occurred to him, he became aware of the change which appeared to have come over his opponent. No longer could he think of Dusty Fog as small, young, or insignificant. Such was the strength of the blond Texan's personality that he seemed to have gained size and heft. Lyle knew that this was purely imaginary, but he could not shake off the illusion.

There, disregarding pure feet and inches, stood a *big*, competent and *very* dangerous *man*.

Dusty Fog was not a reckless boy, hot-headedly trying to avenge a friend and win acclaim for his courage.

He was a *man*—and he knew full well what he was doing!

It was a chilling thought for the Yankee officer.

So much so that Lyle could not make his hand move right then.

"Three!" Billy Jack went on, seeing perspiration forming on Lyle's face.

Looking at Dusty, who was standing apparently relaxed yet gave the impression of being like a compressed spring, just waiting to be released so that he could spring into immediate motion, Lyle began to realize how his own victims had felt. He was facing a man who did not fear him. Who was, in fact, confident of emerging victorious.

Lyle wondered what possible advantage the *big* Texan could have. That he had—or believed he had—one, Lyle did not doubt. No man would dare to stake his life unless he was sure of winning.

Yet, on the face of it, everything appeared to be in Lyle's favour. He had only to drop his hand, lift the revolver, take aim as he squeezed the trigger and fire. Since first deciding upon the duel as a way of removing rivals, he had spent at least fifteen minutes every day in rehearsing the sequence of movements; until he could do them instinctively and without the need for conscious thought.

Against that, Captain Fog would have to reach across, draw a revolver from its holster, cock the hammer and point it in the required direction. It seemed that the Texan had no hope of succeeding.

So why, Lyle asked himself, had Fog insisted upon such terms?

"Four," Billy Jack counted, the words flowing as slowly yet inexorably as the ticking of a clock.

Legends of the speed with which Western gun fighters could draw and shoot had not yet started to circulate, so Lyle had no conception of how fast and deadly a man trained in the frontier fashion of revolver fighting could be. All he knew was that his opponent exuded a quiet, unnerving confidence. There had to be some factor, of which Lyle was unaware, that caused Dusty Fog to feel so sure of victory.

"Five!"

Although Lyle was engrossed in his thoughts, Billy Jack's word triggered off his reflexes. Down swooped his right hand, gathering up the Tranter and starting to raise it to shoulder level.

At the same instant, Dusty's hands passed on their flights across to their waiting Colts. While Lyle's Tranter continued to rise, the Texan's revolvers merely cleared the lips of their holsters and turned the barrels outwards. Back rode the hammers, under his thumbs and his forefingers found the triggers as the weapons lined at waist level.

Suddenly, finding himself confronted by the muzzles of the Colts, Lyle understood where Dusty's advantage had been. The major attempted to halt his instinctive actions, but he was too late.

Flame lashed from the barrels of Dusty's Colts. With twin detonations that merged into a single sound, they drove a pair of .44 bullets into Lyle's left breast. Jerked backwards, the major completed the pressure on the Tranter's trigger, but its bullet winged harmlessly into the ceiling. Stumbling against the table, he bounced from it to the floor.

"Whew!" Billy Jack breathed, advancing from where he had retreated to the side-piece and out of the possible line of fire. "I figured he was going to get you, Cap'n Dusty. Right pleased he didn't."

"And me," the small Texan admitted, holstering the Colts.

"Yes, sir," Billy Jack went on. "Happen he had downed you, I'd've been next to go."

"I'm right pleased to know how concerned you were about *me*," Dusty growled, watching his companion bend over Lyle. "Is he dead?"

"Sure," the sergeant major confirmed. "And I've never seen a man who deserved to die more than him."

"Or me," Dusty agreed. "He caused a lot of people to die and, no matter what I told him, we could never have convicted him for doing it. That's why I faced him down."

"I reckon General Hardin and Colonel Blaze'll claim you did right," Billy Jack drawled. "Give him his due, Cap'n Dusty, he died game."

"We'll give him that," Dusty replied. "Take him to the boat, we'll see he gets a decent burial, even though he didn't give Doug better than being sunk in the lake."

"Yo!" Billy Jack drawled, for they had discovered what had been done with Staunce's body and he knew that the knowledge had steeled Dusty in his resolve to punish Lyle. "How about you?"

"I'll set off the fuses and blow up Big Minnie," Dusty replied.

Fifteen minutes later, Billy Jack and Dusty were supervising the unloading of Lyle's body. There was a shattering roar from the island and the workshop disintegrated. The sound was echoed by two more explosions to the south. The first destroyed Eli Cable's other traction engine.

The second brought a permanent end to the threat of the big gun.